GRAVEYARD
OF DREAMS

SCIENCE FICTION STORIES

GRAVEYARD
OF
DREAMS

SCIENCE
FICTION
STORIES

by

H. BEAM
PIPER

CONTENTS

GRAVEYARD OF DREAMS

Standing at the armor-glass front of the observation deck and watching the mountains rise and grow on the horizon, Conn Maxwell gripped the metal hand-rail with painful intensity, as though trying to hold back the airship by force. Thirty minutes — twenty-six and a fraction of the Terran minutes he had become accustomed to — until he'd have to face it.

Then, realizing that he never, in his own thoughts, addressed himself as "sir," he turned.

"I beg your pardon?"

It was the first officer, wearing a Terran Federation Space Navy uniform of forty years, or about ten regulation-changes, ago. That was the sort of thing he had taken for granted before he had gone away. Now he was noticing it everywhere.

"Thirty minutes out of Litchfield, sir," the ship's officer repeated. "You'll go off by the midship gangway on the starboard side."

"Yes, I know. Thank you."

The first mate held out the clipboard he was carrying. "Would you mind checking over this, Mr. Maxwell? Your baggage list."

"Certainly." He glanced at the slip of paper. Valises, eighteen and twenty-five kilos, two; trunks, seventy-five and seventy kilos, two; microbook case, one-fifty kilos, one. The last item fanned up a little flicker of anger in him, not at any person, even himself, but at the situation in which he found himself and the futility of the whole thing.

"Yes, that's everything. I have no hand-luggage, just

this stuff."

He noticed that this was the only baggage list under the clip; the other papers were all freight and express manifests. "Not many passengers left aboard, are there?"

"You're the only one in first-class, sir," the mate replied. "About forty farm-laborers on the lower deck. Everybody else got off at the other stops. Litchfield's the end of the run. You know anything about the place?"

"I was born there. I've been away at school for the last five years."

"On Baldur?"

"Terra. University of Montevideo." Once Conn would have said it almost boastfully.

The mate gave him a quick look of surprised respect, then grinned and nodded. "Of course; I should have known. You're Rodney Maxwell's son, aren't you? Your father's one of our regular freight shippers. Been sending out a lot of stuff lately." He looked as though he would have liked to continue the conversation, but said: "Sorry, I've got to go. Lot of things to attend to before landing." He touched the visor of his cap and turned away.

The mountains were closer when Conn looked forward again, and he glanced down. Five years and two space voyages ago, seen from the afterdeck of this ship or one of her sisters, the woods had been green with new foliage, and the wine-melon fields had been in pink blossom. He tried to picture the scene sliding away below instead of drawing in toward him, as though to force himself back to a moment of the irretrievable past.

But the moment was gone, and with it the eager excitement and the half-formed anticipations of the things he would learn and accomplish on Terra. The things he would learn — microbook case, one-fifty kilos, one. One of the steel trunks was full of things he had learned and accomplished, too. Maybe they, at least, had some value. . . .

The woods were autumn-tinted now and the fields were bare and brown.

They had gotten the crop in early this year, for the fields had all been harvested. Those workers below must be going out for the wine-pressing. That extra hands were needed for that meant a big crop, and yet it seemed that less land was under cultivation than when he had gone away. He could see squares of low brush among the new forests that had grown up in the last forty years, and the few stands of original timber looked like hills above the second growth. Those trees had been standing when the planet had been colonized.

That had been two hundred years ago, at the middle of the Seventh Century, Atomic Era. The name of the planet — Poictesme — told that: the Surromanticist Movement, when the critics and professors were rediscovering James Branch Cabell.

Funny how much was coming back to him now — things he had picked up from the minimal liberal-arts and general-humanities courses he had taken and then forgotten in his absorption with the science and tech studies.

The first extrasolar planets, as they had been discovered, had been named from Norse mythology — Odin and Baldur and Thor, Uller and Freya, Bifrost and Asgard and Niflheim. When the Norse names ran out, the discoverers had turned to other mythologies, Celtic and Egyptian and Hindu and Assyrian, and by the middle of the Seventh Century they were naming planets for almost anything.

Anything, that is, but actual persons; their names were reserved for stars. Like Alpha Gartner, the sun of Poictesme, and Beta Gartner, a buckshot-sized pink glow in the southeast, and Gamma Gartner, out of sight on the other side of the world, all named for old Genji Gartner, the scholarly and half-piratical adventurer whose ship had been the first to approach the three stars and discover that each of them had planets.

Forty-two planets in all, from a couple of methane-giants on Gamma to airless little things with one-sixth Terran gravity. Alpha II had been the only one in the Trisystem with an oxygen atmosphere and life. So Gartner had landed on it, and named it Poictesme, and the settlement that had grown up around the first landing site had been called Storisende. Thirty years later, Genji Gartner died there, after seeing the camp grow to a metropolis, and was buried under a massive monument.

Some of the other planets had been rich in metals, and mines had been opened, and atmosphere-domed factories and processing plants built. None of them could produce anything but hydroponic and tissue-culture foodstuffs, and natural foods from Poictesme had been less expensive, even on the planets of Gamma and Beta. So Poictesme had concentrated on agriculture and grown wealthy at it.

Then, within fifty years of Genji Gartner's death, the economics of interstellar trade overtook the Trisystem and the mines and factories closed down. It was no longer possible to ship the output to a profitable market in the face of the growing self-sufficiency of the colonial planets and the irreducibly high cost of space-freighting.

Below, the brown fields and the red and yellow woods were merging into a ten-mile-square desert of crumbling concrete — empty and roofless sheds and warehouses and barracks, brush-choked parade grounds and landing fields, airship docks, and even a spaceport. They were more recent, dating from Poictesme's second brief and hectic prosperity, when the Terran Federation's Third Fleet-Army Force had occupied the Gartner Trisystem during the System States War.

Millions of troops had been stationed on or routed through Poictesme; tens of thousands of spacecraft had been based on the Trisystem; the mines and factories had reopened for war production. The Federation had spent trillions of sols on Poictesme, piled up mountains of stores and arms and equipment, left the face of the planet cluttered with installations.

Then, ten years before anybody had expected it, the rebellious System States Alliance had collapsed and the war had ended. The Federation armies had gone home, taking with them the clothes they stood in, their personal weapons and a few souvenirs. Everything else had been left behind; even the most expensive equipment was worth less than the cost of removal.

Ever since, Poictesme had been living on salvage. The uniform the first officer was wearing was forty years old — and it was barely a month out of the original packing. On Terra, Conn had told his friends that his father was a prospector and let them interpret that as meaning an explorer for, say, uranium deposits. Rodney Maxwell found plenty of uranium, but he got it by taking apart the warheads of missiles.

The old replacement depot or classification center or training area or whatever it had been had vanished under the ship now and it was all forest back to the mountains, with an occasional cluster of deserted buildings. From one or two, threads of blue smoke rose — bands of farm tramps, camping on their way from harvest to winepressing. Then the eastern foothills were out of sight and he was looking down on the granite spines of the Calder Range; the valley beyond was sloping away and widening out in the distance, and it was time he began thinking of what to say when he landed. He would have to tell them, of course.

He wondered who would be at the dock to meet him, besides his family. Lynne Fawzi, he hoped. Or did he? Her parents would be with her, and Kurt Fawzi would take the news hardest of any of them, and be the first to blame him because it was bad. The hopes he had built for Lynne and himself would have to be held in abeyance till he saw how her father would regard him now.

But however any of them took it, he would have to tell them the truth.

The ship swept on, tearing through the thin puffs of cloud at ten miles a minute. Six minutes to landing. Five. Four. Then he saw the river bend, glinting redly through the haze in the sunlight; Litchfield was inside it, and he stared waiting for the first glimpse of the city. Three minutes, and the ship began to cut speed and lose altitude. The hot-jets had stopped firing and he could hear the whine of the cold-jet rotors.

Then he could see Litchfield, dominated by the Airport Building, so thick that it looked squat for all its height, like a candle-stump in a puddle of its own grease, the other buildings under their carapace of terraces and landing stages seeming to have flowed away from it. And there was the yellow block of the distilleries, and High Garden Terrace, and the Mall. . . .

At first, in the distance, it looked like a living city. Then, second by second, the stigmata of decay became more and more evident. Terraces empty or littered with rubbish; gardens untended and choked with wild growth; windows staring blindly; walls splotched with lichens and grimy where the rains could not wash them.

For a moment, he was afraid that some disaster, unmentioned in his father's letters, had befallen. Then he realized that the change had not been in Litchfield but in himself. After five years, he was seeing it as it really was. He wondered how his family and his friends would look to him now. Or Lynne.

The ship was coming in over the Mall; he could see the cracked paving sprouting grass, the statues askew on their pedestals, the waterless fountains. He thought for an instant that one of them was playing, and then he saw that what he had taken for spray was dust blowing from the empty basin. There was something about dusty fountains, something he had learned at the University. Oh, yes. One of the Second Century Martian Colonial poets, Eirrarsson, or somebody like that:

The fountains are dusty in the Graveyard of Dreams;
The hinges are rusty and swing with tiny screams.

There was more to it, but he couldn't remember; something about empty gardens under an empty sky. There must have been colonies inside the Sol System, before the Interstellar Era, that hadn't turned out any better than Poictesme. Then he stopped trying to remember as the ship turned toward the Airport Building and a couple of tugs — Terran Federation contragravity tanks, with derrick-booms behind and push-poles where the guns had been — came up to bring her down.

He walked along the starboard promenade to the gangway, which the first mate and a couple of airmen were getting open.

Most of the population of top-level Litchfield was in the crowd on the dock. He recognized old Colonel Zareff, with his white hair and plum-brown skin, and Tom Brangwyn, the town marshal, red-faced and bulking above the others. It took a few seconds for him to pick out his father and mother, and his sister Flora, and then to realize that the handsome young man beside Flora was his brother Charley. Charley had been thirteen when Conn had gone away. And there was Kurt Fawzi, the mayor of Litchfield, and there was Lynne, beside him, her red-lipped face tilted upward with a cloud of bright hair behind it.

He waved to her, and she waved back, jumping in excitement, and then everybody was waving, and they were pushing his family to the front and making way for them.

The ship touched down lightly and gave a lurch as she went off contragravity, and they got the gangway open and the steps swung out, and he started down toward the people who had gathered to greet him.

His father was wearing the same black best-suit he had worn when they had parted five years ago. It had been new then; now it was shabby and had acquired a permanent wrinkle across the right hip, over the pistol-butt. Charley was carrying a gun, too; the belt and holster looked as though he had made them himself. His mother's dress was new and so was Flora's — probably made for the occasion. He couldn't be sure just which of the Terran Federation services had provided the material, but Charley's shirt was Medical Service sterilon.

Ashamed that he was noticing and thinking of such things at a time like this, he clasped his father's hand and kissed his mother and Flora. Everybody was talking at once, saying things that he heard only as happy sounds. His brother's words were the first that penetrated as words.

"You didn't know me," Charley was accusing. "Don't deny it; I saw you standing there wondering if I was Flora's new boy friend or what."

"Well, how in Niflheim'd you expect me to? You've grown up since the last time I saw you. You're looking great, kid!" He caught the gleam of Lynne's golden hair beyond Charley's shoulder and pushed him gently aside. "Lynne!"

"Conn, you look just wonderful!" Her arms were around his neck and she was kissing him. "Am I still your girl, Conn?"

He crushed her against him and returned her kisses, assuring her that she was. He wasn't going to let it make a bit of difference how her father took the news — if she didn't.

She babbled on: "You didn't get mixed up with any of those girls on Terra, did you? If you did, don't tell me about it. All I care about is that you're back. Oh, Conn, you don't know how much I missed you . . . Mother, Dad, doesn't he look just splendid?"

Kurt Fawzi, a little thinner, his face more wrinkled, his hair grayer, shook his hand.

"I'm just as glad to see you as anybody, Conn," he said, "even if I'm not being as demonstrative about it as Lynne. Judge, what do you think of our returned wanderer? Franz, shake hands with him, but save the interview for the *News* for later. Professor, here's one student Litchfield Academy won't need to be ashamed of."

He shook hands with them — old Judge Ledue; Franz Veltrin, the newsman; Professor Kellton; a dozen others, some of whom he had not thought of in five years. They were all cordial and happy — how much, he wondered, because he was their neighbor, Conn Maxwell, Rodney Maxwell's son, home from Terra, and how much because of what they hoped he would tell them? Kurt Fawzi, edging him out of the crowd, was the first to voice that.

"Conn, what did you find out?" he asked breathlessly. "Do you know where it is?"

Conn hesitated, looking about desperately; this was no time to start talking to Kurt Fawzi about it. His father was turning toward him from one side, and from the other Tom Brangwyn and Colonel Zareff were approaching more slowly, the older man leaning on a silver-headed cane.

"Don't bother him about it now, Kurt," Rodney Maxwell scolded the mayor. "He's just gotten off the ship; he hasn't had time to say hello to everybody yet."

"But, Rod, I've been waiting to hear what he's found out ever since he went away," Fawzi protested in a hurt tone.

Brangwyn and Colonel Zareff joined them. They were close friends, probably because neither of them was a native of Poictesme.

The town marshal had always been reticent about his

origins, but Conn guessed it was Hathor. Brangwyn's heavy-muscled body, and his ease and grace in handling it, marked him as a man of a high-gravity planet. Besides, Hathor had a permanent cloud-envelope, and Tom Brangwyn's skin had turned boiled-lobster red under the dim orange sunlight of Alpha Gartner.

Old Klem Zareff never hesitated to tell anybody where he came from — he was from Ashmodai, one of the System States planets, and he had commanded a division that had been blasted down to about regimental strength, in the Alliance army.

"Hello, boy," he croaked, extending a trembling hand. "Glad you're home. We all missed you."

"We sure did, Conn," the town marshal agreed, clasping Conn's hand as soon as the old man had released it. "Find out anything definite?"

Kurt Fawzi looked at his watch. "Conn, we've planned a little celebration for you. We only had since day before yesterday, when the spaceship came into radio range, but we're having a dinner party for you at Senta's this evening."

"You couldn't have done anything I'd have liked better, Mr. Fawzi. I'd have to have a meal at Senta's before really feeling that I'd come home."

"Well, here's what I have in mind. It'll be three hours till dinner's ready. Suppose we all go up to my office in the meantime. It'll give the ladies a chance to go home and fix up for the party, and we can have a drink and a talk."

"You want to do that, Conn?" his father asked, a trifle doubtfully. "If you'd rather go home first . . ."

Something in his father's voice and manner disturbed him vaguely; however, he nodded agreement. After a couple of drinks, he'd be better able to tell them.

"Yes, indeed, Mr. Fawzi," Conn said. "I know you're all anxious, but it's a long story. This'll be a good chance to tell you."

Fawzi turned to his wife and daughter, interrupting

himself to shout instructions to a couple of dockhands who were floating the baggage off the ship on a contra-gravity-lifter. Conn's father had sent Charley off with a message to his mother and Flora.

Conn turned to Colonel Zareff. "I noticed extra workers coming out from the hiring agencies in Storisende, and the crop was all in across the Calders. Big wine-pressing this year?"

"Yes, we're up to our necks in melons," the old planter grumbled. "Gehenna of a big crop. Price'll drop like a brick of collapsium, and this time next year we'll be using brandy to wash our feet in."

"If you can't get good prices, hang onto it and age it. I wish you could see what the bars on Terra charge for a drink of ten-year-old Poictesme."

"This isn't Terra and we aren't selling it by the drink. Only place we can sell brandy is at Storisende spaceport, and we have to take what the trading-ship captains offer. You've been on a rich planet for the last five years, Conn. You've forgotten what it's like to live in a poorhouse. And that's what Poictesme is."

"Things'll be better from now on, Klem," the mayor said, putting one hand on the old man's shoulder and the other on Conn's. "Our boy's home. With what he can tell us, we'll be able to solve all our problems. Come on, let's go up and hear about it."

They entered the wide doorway of the warehouse on the dock-level floor of the Airport Building and crossed to the lift. About a dozen others had joined them, all the important men of Litchfield. Inside, Kurt Fawzi's laborers were floating out cargo for the ship — casks of brandy, of course, and a lot of boxes and crates painted light blue and marked with the wreathed globe of the Terran Federation and the gold triangle of the Third Fleet-Army Force and the eight-pointed red star of Ordnance Service. Long cases of rifles, square boxes of ammunition, machine guns, crated auto-cannon and rockets.

"Where'd that stuff come from?" Conn asked his father. "You dig it up?"

His father chuckled. "That happened since the last time I wrote you. Remember the big underground head-quarters complex in the Calders? Everybody thought it had been all cleaned out years ago. You know, it's never a mistake to take a second look at anything that everybody believes. I found a lot of sealed-off sections over there that had never been entered. This stuff's from one of the headquarters defense armories. I have a gang getting the stuff out. Charley and I flew in after lunch, and I'm going back the first thing tomorrow."

"But there's enough combat equipment on hand to outfit a private army for every man, woman and child on Poictesme!" Conn objected. "Where are we going to sell this?"

"Storisende spaceport. The tramp freighters are buying it for newly colonized planets that haven't been industrialized yet. They don't pay much, but it doesn't cost much to get it out, and I've been clearing about three hundred sols a ton on the spaceport docks. That's not bad, you know."

Three hundred sols a ton. A lifter went by stacked with cases of M-504 submachine guns. Unloaded, one of them weighed six pounds, and even a used one was worth a hundred sols. Conn started to say something about that, but then they came to the lift and were crowding onto it.

He had been in Kurt Fawzi's office a few times, always with his father, and he remembered it as a dim, quiet place of genteel conviviality and rambling conversations, with deep, comfortable chairs and many ashtrays. Fawzi's warehouse and brokerage business, and the airline agency, and the government, such as it was, of Litchfield, combined, made few demands on his time and did not prevent the office from being a favored loafing center for the town's elders. The lights were bright only over the big table that served, among other things, as a desk, and the walls were almost invisible in the shadows.

As they came down the hallway from the lift, everybody had begun speaking more softly. Voices were never loud or excited in Kurt Fawzi's office.

Tom Brangwyn went to the table, taking off his belt and holster and laying his pistol aside. The others, crowding into the room, added their weapons to his.

That was something else Conn was seeing with new eyes. It had been five years since he had carried a gun and he was wondering why any of them bothered. A gun was what a boy put on to show that he had reached manhood, and a man carried for the rest of his life out of habit.

Why, there wouldn't be a shooting a year in Litchfield, if you didn't count the farm tramps and drifters, who kept to the lower level or camped in the empty buildings at the edge of town. Or maybe that was it; maybe Litchfield was peaceful because everybody was armed. It certainly wasn't because of anything the Planetary Government at Storisende did to maintain order.

After divesting himself of his gun, Tom Brangwyn took over the bartending, getting out glasses and filling a pitcher of brandy from a keg in the corner.

"Everybody supplied?" Fawzi was asking. "Well, let's drink to our returned emissary. We're all anxious to hear what you found out, Conn. Gentlemen, here's to our friend Conn Maxwell. Welcome home, Conn!"

"Well, it's wonderful to be back, Mr. Fawzi —"

"No, let's not have any of this mister foolishness! You're one of the gang now. And drink up, everybody. We have plenty of brandy, even if we don't have anything else."

"You telling us, Kurt?" somebody demanded. One of the distillery company; the name would come back to Conn in a moment. "When this crop gets pressed and fermented —"

"When I start pressing, I don't know where in

Gehenna I'm going to vat the stuff till it ferments," Colonel Zareff said. "Or why. You won't be able to handle all of it."

"Now, now!" Fawzi reproved. "Let's not start moaning about our troubles. Not the day Conn's come home. Not when he's going to tell us how to find the Third Fleet-Army Force Brain."

"You *did* find out where the Brain is, didn't you, Conn?" Brangwyn asked anxiously.

That set half a dozen of them off at once. They had all sat down after the toast; now they were fidgeting in their chairs, leaning forward, looking at Conn fixedly.

"What did you find out, Conn?"

"It's still here on Poictesme, isn't it?"

"Did you find out where it is?"

He wanted to tell them in one quick sentence and get it over with. He couldn't, any more than he could force himself to squeeze the trigger of a pistol he knew would blow up in his hand.

"Wait a minute, gentlemen." He finished the brandy, and held out the glass to Tom Brangwyn, nodding toward the pitcher. Even the first drink had warmed him and he could feel the constriction easing in his throat and the lump at the pit of his stomach dissolving. "I hope none of you expect me to spread out a map and show you the cross on it, where the Brain is. I can't. I can't even give the approximate location of the thing."

Much of the happy eagerness drained out of the faces around him. Some of them were looking troubled; Colonel Zareff was gnawing the bottom of his mustache, and Judge Ledue's hand shook as he tried to relight his cigar. Conn stole a quick side-glance at his father; Rodney Maxwell was watching him curiously, as though wondering what he was going to say next.

"But it is still here on Poictesme?" Fawzi questioned. "They didn't take it away when they evacuated, did they?"

Conn finished his second drink. This time he picked

up the pitcher and refilled for himself.

"I'm going to have to do a lot of talking," he said, "and it's going to be thirsty work. I'll have to tell you the whole thing from the beginning, and if you start asking questions at random, you'll get me mixed up and I'll miss the important points."

"By all means!" Judge Ledue told him. "Give it in your own words, in what you think is the proper order."

"Thank you, Judge."

Conn drank some more brandy, hoping he could get his courage up without getting drunk. After all, they had a right to a full report; all of them had contributed something toward sending him to Terra.

"The main purpose in my going to the University was to learn computer theory and practice. It wouldn't do any good for us to find the Brain if none of us are able to use it. Well, I learned enough to be able to operate, program and service any computer in existence, and train assistants. During my last year at the University, I had a part-time paid job programming the big positron-neutrino-photon computer in the astrophysics department. When I graduated, I was offered a position as instructor in positronic computer theory."

"You never mentioned that in your letters, son," his father said.

"It was too late for any letter except one that would come on the same ship I did. Beside, it wasn't very important."

"I think it was." There was a catch in old Professor Kellton's voice. "One of my boys, from the Academy, offered a place on the faculty of the University of Montevideo, on Terra!" He poured himself a second drink, something he almost never did.

"Conn means it wasn't important because it didn't have anything to do with the Brain," Fawzi explained and then looked at Conn expectantly.

All right; now he'd tell them. "I went over all the

records of the Third Fleet-Army Force's occupation of Poictesme that are open to the public. On one pretext or another, I got permission to examine the non-classified files that aren't open to public examination. I even got a few peeps at some of the stuff that's still classified secret. I have maps and plans of all the installations that were built on this planet — literally thousands of them, many still undiscovered. Why, we haven't more than scratched the surface of what the Federation left behind here. For instance, all the important installations exist in duplicate, some even in triplicate, as a precaution against Alliance space attack."

"Space attack!" Colonel Zareff was indignant. "There never was a time when the Alliance could have taken the offensive against Poictesme, even if an offensive outside our own space-area had been part of our policy. We just didn't have the ships. It took over a year to move a million and a half troops from Ashmodai to Marduk, and the fleet that was based on Amaterasu was blasted out of existence in the spaceports and in orbit. Hell, at the time of the sur-render, we didn't have —"

"They weren't taking chances on that, Colonel. But the point I want to make is that with everything I did find, I never found, in any official record, a single word about the giant computer we call the Third Fleet-Army Force Brain."

For a time, the only sound in the room was the tiny insectile humming of the electric clock on the wall. Then Professor Kellton set his glass on the table, and it sounded like a hammer-blow.

"Nothing, Conn?" Kurt Fawzi was incredulous and, for the first time, frightened. The others were exchanging uneasy glances. "But you must have! A thing like that —"

"Of course it would be one of the closest secrets during the war," somebody else said. "But in forty years, you'd expect *something* to leak out."

"Why, *during* the war, it was all through the Third

Force. Even the Alliance knew about it; that's how Klem heard of it."

"Well, Conn couldn't just walk into the secret files and read whatever he wanted to. Just because he couldn't find anything —"

"Don't tell *me* about security!" Klem Zareff snorted. "Certainly they still have it classified; staff-brass'd rather lose an eye than declassify anything. If you'd seen the lengths our staff went to — hell, we lost battles because the staff wouldn't release information the troops in the field needed. I remember once —"

"But there *was* a Brain," Judge Ledue was saying, to reassure himself and draw agreement from the others. "It was capable of combining data, and scanning and evaluating all its positronic memories, and forming association patterns, and reasoning with absolute perfection. It was more than a positronic brain — it was a positronic super-mind."

"We'd have won the war, except for the Brain. We had ninety systems, a hundred and thirty inhabited planets, a hundred billion people — and we were on the defensive in our own space-area! Every move we made was known and anticipated by the Federation. How could they have done that without something like the Brain?"

"Conn, from what you learned of computers, how large a volume of space would you say the Brain would have to occupy?" Professor Kellton asked.

Professor Kellton was the most unworldly of the lot, yet he was asking the most practical question.

"Well, the astrophysics computer I worked with at the University occupies a total of about one million cubic feet," Conn began. This was his chance; they'd take anything he told them about computers as gospel. "It was only designed to handle problems in astrophysics. The Brain, being built for space war, would have to handle any such problem. And if half the stories about the Brain are anywhere near true, it handled any other problem —

mathematical, scientific, political, economic, strategic, psychological, even philosophical and ethical. Well, I'd say that a hundred million cubic feet would be the smallest even conceivable."

They all nodded seriously. They were willing to accept that — or anything else, except one thing.

"Lot of places on this planet where a thing that size could be hidden," Tom Brangwyn said, undismayed. "A planet's a mighty big place."

"It could be under water, in one of the seas," Piet Dawes, the banker, suggested. "An underwater dome city wouldn't be any harder to build than a dome city on a poison-atmosphere planet like Tubal-Cain."

"It might even be on Tubal-Cain," a melon-planter said. "Or Hiawatha, or even one of the Beta or Gamma planets. The Third Force was occupying the whole Trisystem, you know." He thought for a moment. "If I'd been in charge, I'd have put it on one of the moons of Pantagruel."

"But that's clear out in the Alpha System," Judge Ledue objected. "We don't have a spaceship on the planet, certainly nothing with a hyperdrive engine. And it would take a lifetime to get out to the Gamma System and back on reaction drive."

Conn put his empty brandy glass on the table and sat erect. A new thought had occurred to him, chasing out of his mind all the worries and fears he had brought with him all the way from Terra.

"Then we'll have to build a ship," he said calmly. "I know, when the Federation evacuated Poictesme, they took every hyperdrive ship with them. But they had plenty of shipyards and spaceports on this planet, and I have maps showing the location of all of them, and barely a third of them have been discovered so far. I'm sure we can find enough hulks, and enough hyperfield generator parts, to assemble a ship or two, and I know we'll find the same or better on some of the other planets.

"And here's another thing," he added. "When we start looking into some of the dome-city plants on Tubal-Cain and Hiawatha and Moruna and Koshchei, we may find the plant or plants where the components for the Brain were fabricated, and if we do, we may find records of where they were shipped, and that'll be it."

"You're right!" Professor Kellton cried, quivering with excitement. "We've been hunting at random for the Brain, so it would only be an accident if we found it. We'll have to do this systematically, and with Conn to help us — Conn, why not build a computer? I don't mean another Brain; I mean a computer to help us find the Brain."

"We can, but we may not even need to build one. When we get out to the industrial planets, we may find one ready except for perhaps some minor alterations."

"But how are we going to finance all this?" Klem Zareff demanded querulously. "We're poorer than snakes, and even one hyperdrive ship's going to cost like Gehenna."

"I've been thinking about that, Klem," Fawzi said. "If we can find material at these shipyards Conn knows about, most of our expense will be labor. Well, haven't we ten workmen competing for every job? They don't really need money, only the things money can buy. We can raise food on the farms and provide whatever else they need out of Federation supplies."

"Sure. As soon as it gets around that we're really trying to do something about this, everybody'll want in on it," Tom Brangwyn predicted.

"And I have no doubt that the Planetary Government at Storisende will give us assistance, once we show that this is a practical and productive enterprise," Judge Ledue put in. "I have some slight influence with the President and —"

"I'm not too sure we want the Government getting into this," Kurt Fawzi replied. "Give them half a chance and that gang at Storisende'll squeeze us right out."

"We can handle this ourselves," Brangwyn agreed. "And when we get some kind of a ship and get out to the other two systems, or even just to Tubal-Cain or Hiawatha, first thing you know, we'll *be* the Planetary Government."

"Well, now, Tom," Fawzi began piously, "the Brain is too big a thing for a few of us to try to monopolize; it'll be for all Poictesme. Of course, it's only proper that we, who are making the effort to locate it, should have the direction of that effort. . . ."

While Fawzi was talking, Rodney Maxwell went to the table, rummaged his pistol out of the pile and buckled it on. The mayor stopped short.

"You leaving us, Rod?"

"Yes, it's getting late. Conn and I are going for a little walk; we'll be at Senta's in half an hour. The fresh air do both of us good and we have a lot to talk about. After all, we haven't seen each other for over five years."

They were silent, however, until they were away from the Airport Building and walking along High Garden Terrace in the direction of the Mall. Conn was glad; his own thoughts were weighing too heavily within him: I didn't do it. I was going to do it; every minute, I was going to do it, and I didn't, and now it's too late.

"That was quite a talk you gave them, son," his father said. "They believed every word of it. A couple of times, I even caught myself starting to believe it."

Conn stopped short. His father stopped beside him and stood looking at him.

"Why didn't you tell them the truth?" Rodney Maxwell asked.

The question angered Conn. It was what he had been asking himself.

"Why didn't I just grab a couple of pistols off the table and shoot the lot of them?" he retorted. "It would have killed them quicker and wouldn't have hurt as much."

His father took the cigar from his mouth and inspected the tip of it. "The truth must be pretty bad then. There is no Brain. Is that it, son?"

"There never was one. I'm not saying that only because I know it would be impossible to build such a computer. I'm telling you what the one man in the Galaxy who ought to know told me — the man who commanded the Third Force during the War."

"Foxx Travis! I didn't know he was still alive. You actually talked to him?"

"Yes. He's on Luna, keeping himself alive at low gravity. It took me a couple of years, and I was afraid he'd die before I got to him, but I finally managed to see him."

"What did he tell you?"

"That no such thing as the Brain ever existed." They started walking again, more slowly, toward the far edge of the terrace, with the sky red and orange in front of them. "The story was all through the Third Force, but it was just one of those wild tales that get started, nobody knows how, among troops. The High Command never denied or even discouraged it. It helped morale, and letting it leak to the enemy was good psychological warfare."

"Klem Zareff says that everybody in the Alliance army heard of the Brain," his father said. "That was why he came here in the first place." He puffed thoughtfully on his cigar. "You said a computer like the Brain would be an impossibility. Why? Wouldn't it be just another computer, only a lot bigger and a lot smarter?"

"Dad, computermen don't like to hear computers called smart," Conn said. "They aren't. The people who build them are smart; a computer only knows what's fed to it. They can hold more information in their banks than a man can in his memory, they can combine it faster, they don't get tired or absent-minded. But they can't imagine, they can't create, and they can't do anything a human brain can't."

"You know, I'd wondered about just that," said his father. "And none of the histories of the War even as much as mentioned the Brain. And I couldn't see why, after the War, they didn't build dozens of them to handle all these Galactic political and economic problems that nobody seems able to solve. A thing like the Brain wouldn't only be useful for war; the people here aren't trying to find it for war purposes."

"You didn't mention any of these doubts to the others, did you?"

"They were just doubts. You knew for sure, and you couldn't tell them."

"I'd come home intending to — tell them there was no Brain, tell them to stop wasting their time hunting for it and start trying to figure out the answers themselves. But I couldn't. They don't believe in the Brain as a tool, to use; it's a machine god that they can bring all their troubles to. You can't take a thing like that away from people without giving them something better."

"I noticed you suggested building a spaceship and agreed with the professor about building a computer. What was your idea? To take their minds off hunting for the Brain and keep them busy?"

Conn shook his head. "I'm serious about the ship — ships. You and Colonel Zareff gave me that idea."

His father looked at him in surprise. "I never said a word in there, and Klem didn't even once mention —"

"Not in Kurt's office; before we went up from the docks. There was Klem, moaning about a good year for melons as though it were a plague, and you selling arms and ammunition by the ton. Why, on Terra or Baldur or Uller, a glass of our brandy brings more than these freighter-captains give us for a cask, and what do you think a colonist on Agramma, or Sekht, or Hachiman, who has to fight for his life against savages and wild animals, would pay for one of those rifles and a thousand rounds of ammunition?"

His father objected. "We can't base the whole economy of a planet on brandy. Only about ten per cent of the arable land on Poictesme will grow wine-melons. And if we start exporting Federation salvage the way you talk of, we'll be selling pieces instead of job lots. We'll net more, but —"

"That's just to get us started. The ships will be used, after that, to get to Tubal-Cain and Hiawatha and the planets of the Beta and Gamma Systems. What I want to see is the mines and factories reopened, people employed, wealth being produced."

"And where'll we sell what we produce? Remember, the mines closed down because there was no more market."

"No more interstellar market, that's true. But there are a hundred and fifty million people on Poictesme. That's a big enough market and a big enough labor force to exploit the wealth of the Gartner Trisystem. We can have prosperity for everybody on our own resources. Just what do we need that we have to get from outside now?"

His father stopped again and sat down on the edge of a fountain — the same one, possibly, from which Conn had seen dust blowing as the airship had been coming in.

"Conn, that's a dangerous idea. That was what brought on the System States War. The Alliance planets took themselves outside the Federation economic orbit and the Federation crushed them."

Conn swore impatiently. "You've been listening to old Klem Zareff ranting about the Lost Cause and the greedy Terran robber barons holding the Galaxy in economic serfdom while they piled up profits. The Federation didn't fight that war for profits; there weren't any profits to fight for. They fought it because if the System States had won, half of them would be at war among themselves now. Make no mistake about it, politically I'm all for the Federation. But economically, I want to see our people exploiting their own resources for themselves, instead of grieving about lost interstellar trade, and bewailing bumper crops, and searching for a mythical robot god."

"You think, if you can get something like that started, that they'll forget about the Brain?" his father asked skeptically.

"That crowd up in Kurt Fawzi's office? Niflheim, no! They'll go on hunting for the Brain as long as they live, and every day they'll be expecting to find it tomorrow. That'll keep them happy. But they're all old men. The ones I'm interested in are the boys of Charley's age. I'm going to give them too many real things to do — building ships, exploring the rest of the Trisystem, opening mines and factories, producing wealth — for them to get caught in that empty old dream."

He looked down at the dusty fountain on which his father sat. "That ghost-dream haunts this graveyard. I want to give them living dreams that they can make come true."

Conn's father sat in silence for a while, his cigar smoke red in the sunset. "If you can do all that, Conn. . . . You know, I believe you can. I'm with you, as far as I can help, and we'll have a talk with Charley. He's a good boy, Conn, and he has a lot of influence among the other youngsters." He looked at his watch. "We'd better be getting along. You don't want to be late for your own coming-home party."

Rodney Maxwell slid off the edge of the fountain to his feet, hitching at the gunbelt under his coat. Have to dig out his own gun and start wearing it, Conn thought. A man simply didn't go around in public without a gun in Litchfield. It wasn't decent. And he'd be spending a lot of time out in the brush, where he'd really need one.

First thing in the morning, he'd unpack that trunk and go over all those maps. There were half a dozen spaceports and maintenance shops and shipyards within a half-day by airboat, none of which had been looted.

He'd look them all over; that would take a couple of weeks. Pick the best shipyard and concentrate on it. Kurt Fawzi'd be the man to recruit labor. Professor Kellton was a scholar, not a scientist. He didn't know beans about hyperdrive engines, but he knew how to do library research.

They came to the edge of High Garden Terrace at the escalator, long motionless, its moving parts rusted fast, that led down to the Mall, and at the bottom of it was Senta's, the tables under the open sky.

A crowd was already gathering. There was Tom Brangwyn, and there was Kurt Fawzi and his wife, and Lynne. And there was Senta herself, fat and dumpy, in one of her preposterous red-and-purple dresses, bustling about, bubbling happily one moment and screaming invective at some laggard waiter the next.

The dinner, Conn knew, would be the best he had eaten in five years, and afterward they would sit in the dim glow of Beta Gartner, sipping coffee and liqueurs, smoking and talking and visiting back and forth from one table to another, as they always did in the evenings at Senta's. Another bit from Eirrarsson's poem came back to him:

> We sit in the twilight, the shadows among,
> And we talk of the happy days when we were brave and
>   young.

That was for the old ones, for Colonel Zareff and Judge Ledue and Dolf Kellton, maybe even for Tom Brangwyn and Franz Veltrin and for his father. But his brother Charley and the boys of his generation would have a future to talk about. And so would he, and Lynne Fawzi.

GENESIS

Aboard the ship, there was neither day nor night; the hours slipped gently by, as vistas of star-gemmed blackness slid across the visiscreens. For the crew, time had some meaning — one watch on duty and two off. But for the thousand-odd colonists, the men and women who were to be the spearhead of migration to a new and friendlier planet, it had none. They slept, and played, worked at such tasks as they could invent, and slept again, while the huge ship followed her plotted trajectory.

Kalvar Dard, the army officer who would lead them in their new home, had as little to do as any of his followers. The ship's officers had all the responsibility for the voyage, and, for the first time in over five years, he had none at all. He was finding the unaccustomed idleness more wearying than the hectic work of loading the ship before the blastoff from Doorsha. He went over his landing and security plans again, and found no probable emergency unprepared for. Dard wandered about the ship, talking to groups of his colonists, and found morale even better than he had hoped. He spent hours staring into the forward visiscreens, watching the disc of Tareesh, the planet of his destination, grow larger and plainer ahead.

Now, with the voyage almost over, he was in the cargo-hold just aft of the Number Seven bulkhead, with six girls to help him, checking construction material which would be needed immediately after landing. The stuff had all been checked two or three times before, but there was no harm in going over it again. It furnished an occupation to fill in the time; it gave Kalvar Dard an excuse for surrounding himself with half a dozen charming girls, and the girls seemed to enjoy being with him. There was tall blonde Olva, the electromagnetician; pert little Varnis, the machinist's helper; Kyna, the surgeon's-aide; dark-haired Analea; Dorita, the accountant; plump little Eldra, the armament technician. At the moment, they were all sitting on or around the desk in the corner of the store-room, going over the inventory when they were not just gabbling.

"Well, how about the rock-drill bitts?" Dorita was asking earnestly, trying to stick to business. "Won't we need them almost as soon as we're off?"

"Yes, we'll have to dig temporary magazines for our explosives, small-arms and artillery ammunition, and storage-pits for our fissionables and radioactives," Kalvar Dard replied. "We'll have to have safe places for that stuff ready before it can be unloaded; and if we run into hard rock near the surface, we'll have to drill holes for blasting-shots."

"The drilling machinery goes into one of those pre-fabricated sheds," Eldra considered. "Will there be room in it for all the bitts, too?"

Kalvar Dard shrugged. "Maybe. If not, we'll cut poles and build racks for them outside. The bitts are nono-steel; they can be stored in the open."

"If there are poles to cut," Olva added.

"I'm not worrying about that," Kalvar Dard replied. "We have a pretty fair idea of conditions on Tareesh; our astronomers have been making telescopic observations for the past fifteen centuries. There's a pretty big Arctic ice-cap, but it's been receding slowly, with a wide belt of what's believed to be open grassland to the south of it, and a belt of what's assumed to be evergreen forest south of that. We plan to land somewhere in the northern hemisphere, about the grassland-forest line. And since Tareesh is richer in water that Doorsha, you mustn't think of grassland in terms of our wire-grass plains, or forests in terms of our brush thickets. The vegetation should be much more luxuriant."

"If there's such a large polar ice-cap, the summers ought to be fairly cool, and the winters cold," Varnis reasoned. "I'd think that would mean fur-bearing animals. Colonel, you'll have to shoot me something with a nice soft fur; I like furs."

Kalvar Dard chuckled. "Shoot you nothing, you can shoot your own furs. I've seen your carbine and pistol scores," he began.

There was a sudden suck of air, disturbing the papers on the desk. They all turned to see one of the ship's rocket-boat bays open; a young Air Force lieutenant named Seldar Glav, who would be staying on Tareesh with them to pilot their aircraft, emerged from an open airlock.

"Don't tell me you've been to Tareesh and back in that thing," Olva greeted him.

Seldar Glav grinned at her. "I could have been, at that; we're only twenty or thirty planetary calibers away, now. We ought to be entering Tareeshan atmosphere by the middle of the next watch. I was only checking the boats, to make sure they'll be ready to launch. . . . Colonel Kalvar, would you mind stepping over here? There's something I think you should look at, sir."

Kalvar Dard took one arm from around Analea's waist and lifted the other from Varnis' shoulder, sliding off the desk. He followed Glav into the boat-bay; as they went through the airlock, the cheerfulness left the young lieutenant's face.

"I didn't want to say anything in front of the girls, sir," he began, "but I've been checking boats to make sure we can make a quick getaway. Our meteor-security's gone out. The detectors are deader then the Fourth Dynasty, and the blasters won't synchronize. . . . Did you hear a big thump, about a half an hour ago, Colonel?"

"Yes, I thought the ship's labor-crew was shifting heavy equipment in the hold aft of us. What was it, a meteor-hit?"

"It was. Just aft of Number Ten bulkhead. A meteor about the size of the nose of that rocket-boat."

Kalvar Dard whistled softly. "Great Gods of Power! The detectors must be dead, to pass up anything like that. . . . Why wasn't a boat-stations call sent out?"

"Captain Vlazil was unwilling to risk starting a panic, sir," the Air Force officer replied. "Really, I'm exceeding my orders in mentioning it to you, but I thought you should know. . . ."

Kalvar Dard swore. "It's a blasted pity Captain Vlazil didn't try thinking! Gold-braided quarter-wit! Maybe his crew might panic, but my people wouldn't. . . . I'm going to call the control-room and have it out with him. By the Ten Gods . . . !"

He ran through the airlock and back into the hold, starting toward the intercom-phone beside the desk. Before he could reach it, there was another heavy jar, rocking the entire ship. He, and Seldar Glav, who had followed him out of the boat-bay, and the six girls, who had risen on hearing their commander's angry voice, were all tumbled into a heap. Dard surged to his feet, dragging Kyna up along with him; together, they helped the others to rise. The ship was suddenly filled with jangling bells, and the red danger-lights on the ceiling were flashing on and off.

"Attention! Attention!" the voice of some officer in the control-room blared out of the intercom-speaker. "The ship has just been hit by a large meteor! All compartments between bulkheads Twelve and Thirteen are sealed off. All persons between bulkheads Twelve and Thirteen, put on oxygen helmets and plug in at the nearest phone connection. Your air is leaking, and you can't get out, but if you put on oxygen equipment immediately, you'll be all right. We'll get you out as soon as we can, and in any case, we are only a few hours out of Tareeshan atmosphere. All persons in Compartment Twelve, put on. . . ."

Kalvar Dard was swearing evilly. "That does it! That does it for good! . . . Anybody else in this compartment, below the living quarter level?"

"No, we're the only ones," Analea told him.

"The people above have their own boats; they can look after themselves. You girls, get in that boat, in there. Glav, you and I'll try to warn the people above. . . ."

There was another jar, heavier than the one which had preceded it, throwing them all down again. As they rose, a new voice was shouting over the public-address system:

"*Abandon ship! Abandon ship!* The converters are backfiring, and rocket-fuel is leaking back toward the engine-rooms! An explosion is imminent! Abandon ship, all hands!"

Kalvar Dard and Seldar Glav grabbed the girls and literally threw them through the hatch, into the rocket-boat. Dard pushed Glav in ahead of him, then jumped in. Before he had picked himself up, two or three of the girls were at the hatch, dogging the cover down.

"All right, Glav, blast off!" Dard ordered. "We've got to be at least a hundred miles from this ship when she blows, or we'll blow with her!"

"Don't I know!" Seldar Glav retorted over his shoulder, racing for the controls. "Grab hold of something, everybody; I'm going to fire all jets at once!"

An instant later, while Kalvar Dard and the girls clung to stanchions and pieces of fixed furniture, the boat shot forward out of its housing. When Dard's head had cleared, it was in free flight.

"How was that?" Glav yelled. "Everybody all right?" He hesitated for a moment. "I think I blacked out for about ten seconds."

Kalvar Dard looked the girls over. Eldra was using a

corner of her smock to stanch a nosebleed, and Olva had a bruise over one eye. Otherwise, everybody was in good shape.

"Wonder we didn't all black out, permanently," he said. "Well, put on the visiscreens, and let's see what's going on outside. Olva, get on the radio and try to see if anybody else got away."

"Set course for Tareesh?" Glav asked. "We haven't fuel enough to make it back to Doorsha."

"I was afraid of that," Dard nodded. "Tareesh it is; northern hemisphere, daylight side. Try to get about the edge of the temperate zone, as near water as you can. . . ."

2

They were flung off their feet again, this time backward along the boat. As they picked themselves up, Seldar Glav was shaking his head, sadly. "That was the ship going up," he said; "the blast must have caught us dead astern."

"All right." Kalvar Dard rubbed a bruised forehead. "Set course for Tareesh, then cut out the jets till we're ready to land. And get the screens on, somebody; I want to see what's happened."

The screens glowed; then full vision came on. The planet on which they would land loomed huge before them, its north pole toward them, and its single satellite on the port side. There was no sign of any rocket-boat in either side screen, and the rear-view screen was a blur of yellow flame from the jets.

"Cut the jets, Glav," Dard repeated. "Didn't you hear me?"

"But I did, sir!" Seldar Glav indicated the firing-panel. Then he glanced at the rear-view screen. "The gods help us! It's yellow flame; the jets are burning out!"

Kalvar Dard had not boasted idly when he had said

that his people would not panic. All the girls went white, and one or two gave low cries of consternation, but that was all.

"What happens next?" Analea wanted to know. "Do we blow, too?"

"Yes, as soon as the fuel-line burns up to the tanks."

"Can you land on Tareesh before then?" Dard asked.

"I can try. How about the satellite? It's closer."

"It's also airless. Look at it and see for yourself," Kalvar Dard advised. "Not enough mass to hold an atmosphere."

Glav looked at the army officer with new respect. He had always been inclined to think of the Frontier Guards as a gang of scientifically illiterate dirk-and-pistol bravos. He fiddled for a while with instruments on the panel; an automatic computer figured the distance to the planet, the boat's velocity, and the time needed for a landing.

"We have a chance, sir," he said. "I think I can set down in about thirty minutes; that should give us about ten minutes to get clear of the boat, before she blows up."

"All right; get busy, girls," Kalvar Dard said. "Grab everything we'll need. Arms and ammunition first; all of them you can find. After that, warm clothing, bedding, tools and food."

With that, he jerked open one of the lockers and began pulling out weapons. He buckled on a pistol and dagger, and handed other weapon-belts to the girls behind him. He found two of the heavy big-game rifles, and several bandoliers of ammunition for them. He tossed out carbines, and boxes of carbine and pistol cartridges. He found two bomb-bags, each containing six light anti-personnel grenades and a big demolition-bomb. Glancing, now and then, at the forward screen, he caught glimpses of blue sky and green-tinted plains below.

"All right!" the pilot yelled. "We're coming in for a landing! A couple of you stand by to get the hatch open."

There was a jolt, and all sense of movement stopped.

A cloud of white smoke drifted past the screens. The girls got the hatch open; snatching up weapons and bedding-wrapped bundles they all scrambled up out of the boat.

There was fire outside. The boat had come down upon a grassy plain; now the grass was burning from the heat of the jets. One by one, they ran forward along the top of the rocket-boat, jumping down to the ground clear of the blaze. Then, with every atom of strength they possessed, they ran away from the doomed boat.

The ground was rough, and the grass high, impeding them. One of the girls tripped and fell; without pausing, two others pulled her to her feet, while another snatched up and slung the carbine she had dropped. Then, ahead, Kalvar Dard saw a deep gully, through which a little stream trickled.

They huddled together at the bottom of it, waiting, for what seemed like a long while. Then a gentle tremor ran through the ground, and swelled to a sickening, heaving shock. A roar of almost palpable sound swept over them, and a flash of blue-white light dimmed the sun above. The sound, the shock, and the searing light did not pass away at once; they continued for seconds that seemed like an eternity. Earth and stones pelted down around them; choking dust rose. Then the thunder and the earth-shock were over; above, incandescent vapors swirled, and darkened into an overhanging pall of smoke and dust.

For a while, they crouched motionless, too stunned to speak. Then shaken nerves steadied and jarred brains cleared. They all rose weakly. Trickles of earth were still coming down from the sides of the gully, and the little stream, which had been clear and sparkling, was roiled with mud. Mechanically, Kalvar Dard brushed the dust from his clothes and looked to his weapons.

"That was just the fuel-tank of a little Class-3 rocket-boat," he said. "I wonder what the explosion of the ship was like." He thought for a moment before continuing. "Glav, I think I know why our jets burned out. We were stern-on to the ship when she blew; the blast drove our flame right back through the jets."

"Do you think the explosion was observed from Doorsha?" Dorita inquired, more concerned about the practical aspects of the situation. "The ship, I mean. After all, we have no means of communication, of our own."

"Oh, I shouldn't doubt it; there were observatories all around the planet watching our ship," Kalvar Dard said. "They probably know all about it, by now. But if any of you are thinking about the chances of rescue, forget it. We're stuck here."

"That's right. There isn't another human being within fifty million miles," Seldar Glav said. "And that was the first and only space-ship ever built. It took fifty years to build her, and even allowing twenty for research that wouldn't have to be duplicated, you can figure when we can expect another one."

"The answer to that one is, never. The ship blew up in space; fifty years' effort and fifteen hundred people gone, like that." Kalvar Dard snapped his fingers. "So now, they'll try to keep Doorsha habitable for a few more thousand years by irrigation, and forget about immigrating to Tareesh."

"Well, maybe, in a hundred thousand years, our descendants will build a ship and go to Doorsha, then," Olva considered.

"Our descendants?" Eldra looked at her in surprise. "You mean, then . . . ?"

Kyna chuckled. "Eldra, you are an awful innocent, about anything that doesn't have a breech-action or a recoil-mechanism," she said. "Why do you think the women on this expedition outnumbered the men seven to five, and why do you think there were so many obstetricians and pediatricians in the med. staff? We were sent out to put a human population on Tareesh, weren't we? Well, here we are."

"But. . . . Aren't we ever going to . . . ?" Varnis began. "Won't we ever see anybody else, or do anything but just live here, like animals, without machines or ground-cars or aircraft or houses or anything?" Then she began to sob bitterly.

Analea, who had been cleaning a carbine that had gotten covered with loose earth during the explosion, laid it down and went to Varnis, putting her arm around the other girl and comforting her. Kalvar Dard picked up the carbine she had laid down.

"Now, let's see," he began. "We have two heavy rifles, six carbines, and eight pistols, and these two bags of bombs. How much ammunition, counting what's in our belts, do we have?"

They took stock of their slender resources, even Varnis joining in the task, as he had hoped she would. There were over two thousand rounds for the pistols, better than fifteen hundred for the carbines, and four hundred for the two big-game guns. They had some spare clothing, mostly space-suit undergarments, enough bed-robes, one hand-axe, two flashlights, a first-aid kit, and three atomic lighters. Each one had a combat-dagger. There was enough tinned food for about a week.

"We'll have to begin looking for game and edible plants, right away," Glav considered. "I suppose there is game, of some sort; but our ammunition won't last forever."

"We'll have to make it last as long as we can; and we'll have to begin improvising weapons," Dard told him. "Throwing-spears, and throwing-axes. If we can find metal, or any recognizable ore that we can smelt, we'll use that; if not, we'll use chipped stone. Also, we can learn to make snares and traps, after we learn the habits of the animals on this planet. By the time the ammunition's gone, we ought to have learned to do without firearms."

"Think we ought to camp here?"

Kalvar Dard shook his head. "No wood here for fuel, and the blast will have scared away all the game. We'd better go upstream; if we go down, we'll find the water roiled with mud and unfit to drink. And if the game on this planet behave like the game-herds on the wastelands of Doorsha, they'll run for high ground when frightened."

Varnis rose from where she had been sitting. Having mastered her emotions, she was making a deliberate effort to show it.

"Let's make up packs out of this stuff," she suggested. "We can use the bedding and spare clothing to bundle up the food and ammunition."

They made up packs and slung them, then climbed out of the gully. Off to the left, the grass was burning in a wide circle around the crater left by the explosion of the rocket-boat. Kalvar Dard, carrying one of the heavy rifles, took the lead. Beside and a little behind him, Analea walked, her carbine ready. Glav, with the other heavy rifle, brought up in the rear, with Olva covering for him, and between, the other girls walked, two and two.

Ahead, on the far horizon, was a distance-blue line of mountains. The little company turned their faces toward them and moved slowly away, across the empty sea of grass.

3

They had been walking, now, for five years. Kalvar Dard still led, the heavy rifle cradled in the crook of his left arm and a sack of bombs slung from his shoulder, his eyes forever shifting to right and left searching for hidden danger. The clothes in which he had jumped from the rocket-boat were patched and ragged; his shoes had been replaced by high laced buskins of smoke-tanned hide.

He was bearded, now, and his hair had been roughly trimmed with the edge of his dagger.

Analea still walked beside him, but her carbine was slung, and she carried three spears with chipped flint heads; one heavy weapon, to be thrown by hand or used for stabbing, and two light javelins to be thrown with the aid of the hooked throwing-stick Glav had invented. Beside her trudged a four-year old boy, hers and Dard's, and on her back, in a fur-lined net bag, she carried their six-month-old baby.

In the rear, Glav still kept his place with the other big-game gun, and Olva walked beside him with carbine and spears; in front of them, their three-year-old daughter toddled. Between vanguard and rearguard, the rest of the party walked: Varnis, carrying her baby on her back, and Dorita, carrying a baby and leading two other children. The baby on her back had cost the life of Kyna in child-birth; one of the others had been left motherless when Eldra had been killed by the Hairy People.

That had been two years ago, in the winter when they had used one of their two demolition-bombs to blast open a cavern in the mountains. It had been a hard winter; two children had died, then — Kyna's firstborn, and the little son of Kalvar Dard and Dorita. It had been their first encounter with the Hairy People, too.

Eldra had gone outside the cave with one of the skin water-bags, to fill it at the spring. It had been after sunset, but she had carried her pistol, and no one had thought of danger until they heard the two quick shots, and the scream. They had all rushed out, to find four shaggy, manlike things tearing at Eldra with hands and teeth, another lying dead, and a sixth huddled at one side, clutching its abdomen and whimpering. There had been a quick flurry of shots that had felled all four of the assail-ants, and Seldar Glav had finished the wounded creature with his dagger, but Eldra was dead. They had built a cairn of stones over her body, as they had done over the bodies of the two children killed by the cold. But, after an examination to see what sort of things they were, they had tumbled the bodies of the Hairy People over the cliff. These had been too bestial to bury as befitted human dead, but too manlike to skin and eat as game.

Since then, they had often found traces of the Hairy People, and when they met with them, they killed them without mercy. These were great shambling parodies of humanity, long-armed, short-legged, twice as heavy as men, with close-set reddish eyes and heavy bone-crushing jaws. They may have been incredibly debased humans, or perhaps beasts on the very threshold of manhood. From what he had seen of conditions on this planet, Kalvar Dard suspected the latter to be the case. In a million or so years, they might evolve into something like humanity. Already, the Hairy ones had learned the use of fire, and of chipped crude stone implements — mostly heavy triangular choppers to be used in the hand, without helves.

Twice, after that night, the Hairy People had attacked them — once while they were on the march, and once in camp. Both assaults had been beaten off without loss to themselves, but at cost of precious ammunition. Once they had caught a band of ten of them swimming a river on logs; they had picked them all off from the bank with their carbines. Once, when Kalvar Dard and Analea had been scouting alone, they had come upon a dozen of them huddled around a fire and had wiped them out with a single grenade. Once, a large band of Hairy People hunted them for two days, but only twice had they come close, and both times, a single shot had sent them all scampering. That had been after the bombing of the group around the fire. Dard was convinced that the beings possessed the rudiments of a language, enough to communicate a few simple ideas, such as the fact that this little tribe of aliens were dangerous in the extreme.

There were Hairy People about now; for the past five days, moving northward through the forest to the open grasslands, the people of Kalvar Dard had found traces of them. Now, as they came out among the seedling growth at the edge of the open plains, everybody was on the alert.

They emerged from the big trees and stopped among the young growth, looking out into the open country. About a mile away, a herd of game was grazing slowly westward. In the distance, they looked like the little horselike things, no higher than a man's waist and heavily maned and bearded, that had been one of their most important sources of meat. For the ten thousandth time, Dard wished, as he strained his eyes, that somebody had thought to secure a pair of binoculars when they had abandoned the rocket-boat. He studied the grazing herd for a long time.

The seedling pines extended almost to the game-herd and would offer concealment for the approach, but the animals were grazing into the wind, and their scent was much keener than their vision. This would prelude one of their favorite hunting techniques, that of lurking in the high grass ahead of the quarry. It had rained heavily in the past few days, and the undermat of dead grass was soaked, making a fire-hunt impossible. Kalvar Dard knew that he could stalk to within easy carbine-shot, but he was unwilling to use cartridges on game; and in view of the proximity of Hairy People, he did not want to divide his band for a drive hunt.

"What's the scheme?" Analea asked him, realizing the problem as well as he did. "Do we try to take them from behind?"

"We'll take them from an angle," he decided. "We'll start from here and work in, closing on them at the rear of the herd. Unless the wind shifts on us, we ought to get within spear-cast. You and I will use the spears; Varnis can come along and cover for us with a carbine. Glav, you and Olva and Dorita stay here with the children and the packs. Keep a sharp lookout; Hairy People around, somewhere." He unslung his rifle and exchanged it for Olva's spears. "We can only eat about two of them before the meat begins to spoil, but kill all you can," he told Analea; "we need the skins."

Then he and the two girls began their slow, cautious, stalk. As long as the grassland was dotted with young trees, they walked upright, making good time, but the last five hundred yards they had to crawl, stopping often to check the wind, while the horse-herd drifted slowly by. Then they were directly behind the herd, with the wind in their faces, and they advanced more rapidly.

"Close enough?" Dard whispered to Analea.

"Yes; I'm taking the one that's lagging a little behind."

"I'm taking the one on the left of it." Kalvar Dard fitted a javelin to the hook of his throwing-stick. "Ready? Now!"

He leaped to his feet, drawing back his right arm and hurling, the throwing-stick giving added velocity to the spear. Beside him, he was conscious of Analea rising and propelling her spear. His missile caught the little bearded pony in the chest; it stumbled and fell forward to its front knees. He snatched another light spear, set it on the hook of the stick and darted it at another horse, which reared, biting at the spear with its teeth. Grabbing the heavy stabbing-spear, he ran forward, finishing it off with a heart-thrust. As he did, Varnis slung her carbine, snatched a stone-headed throwing axe from her belt, and knocked down another horse, then ran forward with her dagger to finish it.

By this time, the herd, alarmed, had stampeded and was galloping away, leaving the dead and dying behind. He and Analea had each killed two; with the one Varnis had knocked down, that made five. Using his dagger, he finished off one that was still kicking on the ground, and then began pulling out the throwing-spears. The girls, shouting in unison, were announcing the successful completion of the hunt; Glav, Olva, and Dorita were coming forward with the children.

It was sunset by the time they had finished the work of skinning and cutting up the horses and had carried the hide-wrapped bundles of meat to the little brook where they had intended camping. There was firewood to be gathered, and the meal to be cooked, and they were all tired.

"We can't do this very often, any more," Kalvar Dard told them, "but we might as well, tonight. Don't bother rubbing sticks for fire; I'll use the lighter."

He got it from a pouch on his belt — a small, gold-plated, atomic lighter, bearing the crest of his old regiment of the Frontier Guards. It was the last one they had, in working order. Piling a handful of dry splinters under the firewood, he held the lighter to it, pressed the activator, and watched the fire eat into the wood.

The greatest achievement of man's civilization, the mastery of the basic, cosmic, power of the atom — being used to kindle a fire of natural fuel, to cook unseasoned meat killed with stone-tipped spears. Dard looked sadly at the twinkling little gadget, then slipped it back into its pouch. Soon it would be worn out, like the other two, and then they would gain fire only by rubbing dry sticks, or hacking sparks from bits of flint or pyrites. Soon, too, the last cartridge would be fired, and then they would perforce depend for protection, as they were already doing for food, upon their spears.

And they were so helpless. Six adults, burdened with seven little children, all of them requiring momently care and watchfulness. If the cartridges could be made to last until they were old enough to fend for themselves. . . . If they could avoid collisions with the Hairy People. . . . Some day, they would be numerous enough for effective mutual protection and support; some day, the ratio of helpless children to able adults would redress itself. Until then, all that they could do would be to survive; day after day, they must follow the game-herds.

4

For twenty years, now, they had been following the game. Winters had come, with driving snow, forcing horses and deer into the woods, and the little band of humans to the protection of mountain caves. Springtime followed, with fresh grass on the plains and plenty of meat for the people of Kalvar Dard. Autumns followed summers, with fire-hunts, and the smoking and curing of meat and hides. Winters followed autumns, and springtimes came again, and thus until the twentieth year after the landing of the rocket-boat.

Kalvar Dard still walked in the lead, his hair and beard flecked with gray, but he no longer carried the heavy rifle; the last cartridge for that had been fired long ago. He carried the hand-axe, fitted with a long helve, and a spear with a steel head that had been worked painfully from the receiver of a useless carbine. He still had his pistol, with eight cartridges in the magazine, and his dagger, and the bomb-bag, containing the big demolition-bomb and one grenade. The last shred of clothing from the ship was gone, now; he was clad in a sleeveless tunic of skin and horsehide buskins.

Analea no longer walked beside him; eight years before, she had broken her back in a fall. It had been impossible to move her, and she stabbed herself with her dagger to save a cartridge. Seldar Glav had broken through the ice while crossing a river, and had lost his rifle; the next day he died of the chill he had taken. Olva had been killed by the Hairy People, the night they had attacked the camp, when Varnis' child had been killed.

They had beaten off that attack, shot or speared ten of

the huge sub-men, and the next morning they buried their dead after their custom, under cairns of stone. Varnis had watched the burial of her child with blank, uncomprehending eyes, then she had turned to Kalvar Dard and said something that had horrified him more than any wild outburst of grief could have.

"Come on, Dard; what are we doing this for? You promised you'd take us to Tareesh, where we'd have good houses, and machines, and all sorts of lovely things to eat and wear. I don't like this place, Dard; I want to go to Tareesh."

From that day on, she had wandered in merciful darkness. She had not been idiotic, or raving mad; she had just escaped from a reality that she could no longer bear.

Varnis, lost in her dream-world, and Dorita, hard-faced and haggard, were the only ones left, beside Kalvar Dard, of the original eight. But the band had grown, meanwhile, to more than fifteen. In the rear, in Seldar Glav's old place, the son of Kalvar Dard and Analea walked. Like his father, he wore a pistol, for which he had six rounds, and a dagger, and in his hand he carried a stone-headed killing-maul with a three-foot handle which he had made for himself. The woman who walked beside him and carried his spears was the daughter of Glav and Olva; in a net-bag on her back she carried their infant child. The first Tareeshan born of Tareeshan parents; Kalvar Dard often looked at his little grandchild during nights in camp and days on the trail, seeing, in that tiny fur-swaddled morsel of humanity, the meaning and purpose of all that he did. Of the older girls, one or two were already pregnant, now; this tiny threatened beach-head of humanity was expanding, gaining strength. Long after man had died out on Doorsha and the dying planet itself had become an arid waste, the progeny of this little band would continue to grow and to dominate the younger planet, nearer the sun. Some day, an even

mightier civilization than the one he had left would rise
here. . . .

All day the trail had wound upward into the mountains. Great cliffs loomed above them, and little
streams spumed and dashed in rocky gorges below. All
day, the Hairy People had followed, fearful to approach
too close, unwilling to allow their enemies to escape. It
had started when they had rushed the camp, at daybreak;
they had been beaten off, at cost of almost all the ammunition, and the death of one child. No sooner had the
tribe of Kalvar Dard taken the trail, however, than they
had been pressing after them. Dard had determined to
cross the mountains, and had led his people up a game-
trail, leading toward the notch of a pass high against the
skyline.

The shaggy ape-things seemed to have divined his
purpose. Once or twice, he had seen hairy brown shapes
dodging among the rocks and stunted trees to the left.
They were trying to reach the pass ahead of him. Well, if
they did. . . . He made a quick mental survey of his
resources. His pistol, and his son's, and Dorita's, with
eight, and six, and seven rounds. One grenade, and the
big demolition bomb, too powerful to be thrown by hand,
but which could be set for delayed explosion and dropped
over a cliff or left behind to explode among pursuers. Five
steel daggers, and plenty of spears and slings and axes.
Himself, his son and his son's woman, Dorita, and four or
five of the older boys and girls, who would make effective
front-line fighters. And Varnis, who might come out of
her private dream-world long enough to give account for
herself, and even the tiniest of the walking children could
throw stones or light spears. Yes, they could force the
pass, if the Hairy People reached it ahead of them, and
then seal it shut with the heavy bomb. What lay on the
other side, he did not know; he wondered how much

game there would be, and if there were Hairy People on that side, too.

Two shots slammed quickly behind him. He dropped his axe and took a two-hand grip on his stabbing-spear as he turned. His son was hurrying forward, his pistol drawn, glancing behind as he came.

"Hairy People. Four," he reported. "I shot two; she threw a spear and killed another. The other ran."

The daughter of Seldar Glav and Olva nodded in agreement.

"I had no time to throw again," she said, "and Bo-Bo would not shoot the one that ran."

Kalvar Dard's son, who had no other name than the one his mother had called him as a child, defended himself. "He was running away. It is the rule: *use bullets only to save life, where a spear will not serve.*"

Kalvar Dard nodded. "You did right, son," he said, taking out his own pistol and removing the magazine, from which he extracted two cartridges. "Load these into your pistol; four rounds aren't enough. Now we each have six. Go back to the rear, keep the little ones moving, and don't let Varnis get behind."

"That is right. *We must all look out for Varnis, and take care of her,*" the boy recited obediently. "That is the rule."

He dropped to the rear. Kalvar Dard holstered his pistol and picked up his axe, and the column moved forward again. They were following a ledge, now; on the left, there was a sheer drop of several hundred feet, and on the right a cliff rose above them, growing higher and steeper as the trail slanted upward. Dard was worried about the ledge; if it came to an end, they would all be trapped. No one would escape. He suddenly felt old and unutterably weary. It was a frightful weight that he bore — responsibility for an entire race.

Suddenly, behind him, Dorita fired her pistol upward. Dard sprang forward — there was no room for him to jump aside — and drew his pistol. The boy, Bo-Bo, was trying to find a target from his position in the rear. Then Dard saw the two Hairy People; the boy fired, and the stone fell, all at once.

It was a heavy stone, half as big as a man's torso, and it almost missed Kalvar Dard. If it had hit him directly, it would have killed him instantly, mashing him to a bloody pulp; as it was, he was knocked flat, the stone pinning his legs.

At Bo-Bo's shot, a hairy body plummeted down to hit the ledge. Bo-Bo's woman instantly ran it through with one of her spears. The other ape-thing, the one Dorita had shot, was still clinging to a rock above. Two of the children scampered up to it and speared it repeatedly, screaming like little furies. Dorita and one of the older girls got the rock off Kalvar Dard's legs and tried to help him to his feet, but he collapsed, unable to stand. Both his legs were broken.

This was it, he thought, sinking back.

"Dorita, I want you to run ahead and see what the trail's like," he said. "See if the ledge is passable. And find a place, not too far ahead, where we can block the trail by exploding that demolition-bomb. It has to be close enough for a couple of you to carry or drag me and get me there in one piece."

"What are you going to do?"

"What do you think?" he retorted. "I have both legs broken. You can't carry me with you; if you try it, they'll catch us and kill us all. I'll have to stay behind; I'll block the trail behind you, and get as many of them as I can while I'm at it. Now, run along and do as I said."

She nodded. "I'll be back as soon as I can," she agreed.

The others were crowding around Dard. Bo-Bo bent over him, perplexed and worried. "What are you going to do, father?" he asked. "You are hurt. Are you going to go away and leave us, as mother did when she was hurt?"

"Yes, son; I'll have to. You carry me on ahead a little, when Dorita gets back, and leave me where she shows you to. I'm going to stay behind and block the trail, and kill a few Hairy People. I'll use the big bomb."

"The *big* bomb? The one nobody dares throw?" The boy looked at his father in wonder.

"That's right. Now, when you leave me, take the others and get away as fast as you can. Don't stop till you're up to the pass. Take my pistol and dagger, and the axe and the big spear, and take the little bomb, too. Take everything I have, only leave the big bomb with me. I'll need that."

Dorita rejoined them. "There's a waterfall ahead. We can get around it, and up to the pass. The way's clear and easy; if you put off the bomb just this side of it, you'll start a rock-slide that'll block everything."

"All right. Pick me up, a couple of you. Don't take hold of me below the knees. And hurry."

A hairy shape appeared on the ledge below them; one of the older boys used his throwing-stick to drive a javelin into it. Two of the girls picked up Dard; Bo-Bo and his woman gathered up the big spear and the axe and the bomb-bag.

They hurried forward, picking their way along the top of a talus of rubble at the foot of the cliff, and came to where the stream gushed out of a narrow gorge. The air was wet with spray there, and loud with the roar of the waterfall. Kalvar Dard looked around; Dorita had chosen the spot well. Not even a sure-footed mountain-goat could make the ascent, once that gorge was blocked.

"All right; put me down here," he directed. "Bo-Bo, take my belt, and give me the big bomb. You have one light grenade; know how to use it?"

"Of course, you have often showed me. I turn the top, and then press in the little thing on the side, and hold it in till I throw. I throw it at least a spear-cast, and drop to the ground or behind something."

"That's right. And use it only in greatest danger, to save everybody. Spare your cartridges; use them only to save life. And save everything of metal, no matter how small."

"Yes. Those are the rules. I will follow them, and so will the others. And we will always take care of Varnis."

"Well, goodbye, son." He gripped the boy's hand. "Now get everybody out of here; don't stop till you're at the pass."

"You're not staying behind!" Varnis cried. "Dard, you promised us! I remember, when we were all in the ship together — you and I and Analea and Olva and Dorita and Eldra and, oh, what was that other girl's name, Kyna! And we were all having such a nice time, and you were telling us how we'd all come to Tareesh, and we were having such fun talking about it. . . ."

"That's right, Varnis," he agreed. "And so I will. I have something to do, here, but I'll meet you on top of the mountain, after I'm through, and in the morning we'll all go to Tareesh."

She smiled — the gentle, childlike smile of the harmlessly mad — and turned away. The son of Kalvar Dard made sure that she and all the children were on the way, and then he, too, turned and followed them, leaving Dard alone.

Alone, with a bomb and a task. He'd borne that task for twenty years, now; in a few minutes, it would be ended, with an instant's searing heat. He tried not to be too glad; there were so many things he might have done, if he had tried harder. Metals, for instance. Somewhere there surely must be ores which they could have smelted, but he had never found them. And he might have tried catching some of the little horses they hunted for food, to break and train to bear burdens. And the alphabet — why hadn't he taught it to Bo-Bo and the daughter of Seldar Glav, and laid on them an obligation to teach the others?

And the grass-seeds they used for making flour sometimes; they should have planted fields of the better kinds, and patches of edible roots, and returned at the proper time to harvest them. There were so many things, things that none of those young savages or their children would think of in ten thousand years. . . .

Something was moving among the rocks, a hundred yards away. He straightened, as much as his broken legs would permit, and watched. Yes, there was one of them, and there was another, and another. One rose from behind a rock and came forward at a shambling run, making bestial sounds. Then two more lumbered into sight, and in a moment the ravine was alive with them. They were almost upon him when Kalvar Dard pressed in the thumbpiece of the bomb; they were clutching at him when he released it. He felt a slight jar. . . .

When they reached the pass, they all stopped as the son of Kalvar Dard turned and looked back. Dorita stood beside him, looking toward the waterfall too; she also knew what was about to happen. The others merely gaped in blank incomprehension, or grasped their weapons, thinking that the enemy was pressing close behind and that they were making a stand here. A few of the smaller boys and girls began picking up stones.

Then a tiny pin-point of brilliance winked, just below where the snow-fed stream vanished into the gorge. That was all, for an instant, and then a great fire-shot cloud swirled upward, hundreds of feet into the air; there was a crash, louder than any sound any of them except Dorita and Varnis had ever heard before.

"He did it!" Dorita said softly.

"Yes, he did it. My father was a brave man," Bo-Bo replied. "We are safe, now."

Varnis, shocked by the explosion, turned and stared at him, and then she laughed happily. "Why, there you are, Dard!" she exclaimed. "I was wondering where you'd gone. What did you do after we left?"

"What do you mean?" The boy was puzzled, not knowing how much he looked like his father, when his father had been an officer of the Frontier Guards, twenty years before.

His puzzlement worried Varnis vaguely. "You. . . . You are Dard, aren't you?" she asked. "But that's silly; of course you're Dard! Who else could you be?"

"Yes. I am Dard," the boy said, remembering that it was the rule for everybody to be kind to Varnis and to pretend to agree with her. Then another thought struck him. His shoulders straightened. "Yes. I am Dard, son of Dard," he told them all. "I lead, now. Does anybody say no?"

He shifted his axe and spear to his left hand and laid his right hand on the butt of his pistol, looking sternly at Dorita. If any of them tried to dispute his claim, it would be she. But instead, she gave him the nearest thing to a real smile that had crossed her face in years.

"You are Dard," she told him; "you lead us, now."

"But of course Dard leads! Hasn't he always led us?" Varnis wanted to know. "Then what's all the argument about? And tomorrow he's going to take us to Tareesh, and we'll have houses and ground-cars and aircraft and gardens and lights, and all the lovely things we want. Aren't you, Dard?"

"Yes, Varnis; I will take you all to Tareesh, to all the wonderful things," Dard, son of Dard, promised, for such was the rule about Varnis.

Then he looked down from the pass into the country beyond. There were lower mountains, below, and foot-hills, and a wide blue valley, and, beyond that, distant peaks reared jaggedly against the sky. He pointed with his father's axe.

"We go down that way," he said.

So they went, down, and on, and on, and on. The last cartridge was fired; the last sliver of Doorshan metal wore out or rusted away. By then, however, they had learned to make chipped stone, and bone, and reindeer-horn serve their needs. Century after century, millennium after millennium, they followed the game-herds from birth to death, and birth replenished their numbers faster than death depleted. Bands grew in numbers and split; young men rebelled against the rule of the old and took their women and children elsewhere.

They hunted down the hairy Neanderthalers, and exterminated them ruthlessly, the origin of their implacable hatred lost in legend. All that they remembered, in the misty, confused, way that one remembers a dream, was that there had once been a time of happiness and plenty, and that there was a goal to which they would some day attain. They left the mountains — were they the Caucasus? The Alps? The Pamirs? — and spread outward, conquering as they went.

We find their bones, and their stone weapons, and their crude paintings, in the caves of Cro-Magnon and Grimaldi and Altimira and Mas-d'Azil; the deep layers of horse and reindeer and mammoth bones at their feasting-place at Solutre. We wonder how and whence a race so like our own came into a world of brutish sub-humans.

Just as we wonder, too, at the network of canals which radiate from the polar caps of our sister planet, and speculate on the possibility that they were the work of hands like our own. And we concoct elaborate jokes about the "Men From Mars" — *ourselves.*

OPERATION R.S.V.P

Vladmir N. Dzhoubinsky, Foreign Minister, Union of East European Soviet Republics, to Wu Fung Tung, Foreign Minister, United Peoples' Republics of East Asia:

15 Jan. 1984
Honored Sir:

Pursuant to our well known policy of exchanging military and scientific information with the Government, of friendly Powers, my Government takes great pleasure in announcing the completely successful final tests of our new nuclear-rocket guided missile Marxist Victory. The test launching was made from a position south of Lake Balkash; the target was located in the East Siberian Sea.

In order to assist you in appreciating the range of the new guided missile Marxist Victory, let me point out that the distance from launching-site to target is somewhat over 50 percent greater than the distance from launching-site to your capital, Nanking.

My Government is still hopeful that your Government will revise its present intransigeant position on the Khakum River dispute.

I have the honor, etc., etc., etc.,

V. N. Dzhoubinsky

✳   ✳   ✳

Wu Fung Tung, to Vladmir N. Dzhoubinsky:

7 Feb., 1984
Estimable Sir:

My Government was most delighted to learn of the splendid triumph of your Government in developing the new guided missile Marxist Victory, and at the same time deeply relieved. We had, of course, detected the release of nuclear energy incident to the test, and inasmuch as it had obviously originated in the disintegration of a quantity of Uranium 235, we had feared that an explosion had occurred at your Government's secret uranium plant at Khatanga. We have long known of the lax security measures in effect at this plant, and have, as a consequence, been expecting some disaster there.

I am therefore sure that your Government will be equally gratified to learn of the perfection, by my Government, of our own new guided missile Celestial Destroyer, which embodies, in greatly improved form, many of the features of your own Government's guided missile Marxist Victory. Naturally, your own scientific warfare specialists have detected the release of energy incident to the explosion of our own improved thorium-hafnium interaction bomb; this bomb was exploded over the North Polar ice cap, about two hundred miles south of the Pole, on about 35 degrees East Longitude, almost due north of your capital city of Moscow. The launching was made from a site in Thibet.

Naturally, my Government cannot deviate from our present just and reasonable attitude in the Khakum River question. Trusting that your Government will realize this, I have the honor to be,

Your obedient and respectful servant,
Wu Fung Tung

*　　　*　　　*

From *N. Y. Times*, Feb. 20, 1984:

AFGHAN RULER FÊTED AT NANKING
Ameer Shere Ali Abdallah Confers
with
UPREA Pres. Sung Li-Yin

UEESR Foreign Minister Dzhoubinsky to Maxim G. Krylenkoff, Ambassador at Nanking:

3 March, 1984
Comrade Ambassador:
It is desired that you make immediate secret and confidential repeat secret and confidential inquiry as to the whereabouts of Dr. Dimitri O. Voronoff, the noted Soviet rocket expert, designer of the new guided missile Marxist Victory, who vanished a week ago from the Josef Vissarionovitch Djugashvli Reaction-Propulsion Laboratories at Molotovgorod. It is feared in Government circles that this noted scientist has been abducted by agents of the United Peoples' Republics of East Asia, possibly to extract from him, under torture, information of a secret technical nature.

As you know, this is but the latest of a series of such disappearances, beginning about five years ago, when the Khakum River question first arose.

Your utmost activity in this matter is required.
Dzhoubinsky

❋   ❋   ❋

Ambassador Krylenkoff to Foreign Minister Dzhoubinsky:

9 March, 1984
Comrade Foreign Minister:
Since receipt of yours of 3/3/'84, I have been utilizing all resources at my disposal in the matter of the noted sci-

entist D. O. Voronoff, and availing myself of all sources of information, e.g., spies, secret agents, disaffected elements of the local population, and including two UPREA Cabinet Ministers on my payroll. I regret to report that results of this investigation have been entirely negative. No one here appears to know anything of the whereabouts of Dr. Voronoff.

At the same time, there is considerable concern in UPREA Government circles over the disappearances of certain prominent East Asian scientists, e.g.. Dr. Hong Foo, the nuclear physicist; Dr. Hin Yang-Woo, the great theoretical mathematician; Dr. Mong Shing, the electronics expert. I am informed that UPREA Government sources are attributing these disappearances to us.

I can only say that I am sincerely sorry that this is not the case.

Krylenkoff

＊　　　＊　　　＊

Wu Fung Tung to Vladmir N. Dzhoubinsky:

21 April, 1984
Estimable Sir:

In accordance with our established policy of free exchange with friendly Powers of scientific information, permit me to inform your Government that a new mutated disease-virus has been developed in our biological laboratories, causing a highly contagious disease similar in symptoms to bubonic plague, but responding to none of the treatments for this latter disease. This new virus strain was accidentally produced in the course of some experiments with radioactivity.

In spite of the greatest care, it is feared that this virus has spread beyond the laboratory in which it was developed. We warn you most urgently of the danger that it may have spread to the UEESR; enclosed are a list of symptoms, etc.

My Government instructs me to advise your Government that the attitude of your Government in the Khakum River question is utterly unacceptable, and will require considerable revision before my Government can even consider negotiation with your Government on the subject. Your obedient and respectful servant,

Wu Fung Tung

✳   ✳   ✳

From *N. Y. Times*, May 12, 1984:

AFGHAN RULER FÊTED AT MOSCOW
Ameer sees Red Square Troop Review;
Confers with Premier-President Mouzorgin

✳   ✳   ✳

Sing Yat, UPREA Ambassador at Moscow, to Wu Fung Tung:

26 June, 1984

Venerable and Honored Sir:

I regret humbly that I can learn nothing whatever about the fate of the learned scholars of science of whom you inquire, namely: Hong Foo, Hin Yang-Woo, Mong Shing, Yee Ho Li, Wong Fat, and Bao Hu-Shin. This inability may be in part due to incompetence of my unworthy self, but none of my many sources of information, including Soviet Minister of Police Morgodoff, who is on my payroll, can furnish any useful data whatever. I am informed, however, that the UEESR Government is deeply concerned about similar disappearances of some of the foremost of their own scientists, including Voronoff, Jirnikov, Kagorinoff, Bakhorin, Himmelfarber and Pavlovinsky, all of whose dossiers are on file with our Bureau of Foreign Intelligence. I am further informed that the Government of the UEESR ascribes these disappearances to our own activities.

Ah, Venerable and Honored Sir, if this were only true!
Kindly condescend to accept compliments of,
Sing Yat

*   *   *

Dzhoubinsky to Wu Fung Tung:

6 October, 1984
Honored Sir:

Pursuant to our well known policy of exchanging scientific information with the Governments of friendly Powers, my Government takes the greatest pleasure in announcing a scientific discovery of inestimable value to the entire world. I refer to nothing less than a positive technique for liquidating rats as a species.

This technique involves treatment of male rats with certain types of hard radiations, which not only renders them reproductively sterile but leaves the rodents so treated in full possession of all other sexual functions and impulses. Furthermore, this condition of sterility is venereally contagious, so that one male rat so treated will sterilize all female rats with which it comes in contact, and these, in turn, will sterilize all male rats coming in contact with them. Our mathematicians estimate that under even moderately favorable circumstances, the entire rat population of the world could be sterilized from one male rat in approximately two hundred years.

Rats so treated have already been liberated in the granaries at Odessa; in three months, rat-trappings there have fallen by 26.4 percent, and grain-losses to rats by 32.09 percent.

We are shipping you six dozen sterilized male rats, which you can use for sterilization stock, and, by so augmenting their numbers, may duplicate our own successes.

Curiously enough, this effect of venereally contagious sterility was discovered quite accidentally, in connection with the use of hard radiations for human sterilization (criminals, mental defectives, etc.). Knowing the disastrous possible effects of an epidemic of contagious human sterility, all persons so sterilized were liquidated as soon as the contagious nature of their sterility had been discovered, with the exception of a dozen or so convicts, who had been released before this discovery was made. It is believed that at least some of them have made their way over the border and into the territory of the United Peoples' Republics of East Asia. I must caution your Government to be on the lookout of them. Among a people still practicing ancestor-worship, an epidemic of sterility would be a disaster indeed.

My Government must insist that your Government take some definite step toward the solution of the Khakum River question; the present position of the Government of the United Peoples' Republics of East Asia on this subject is utterly unacceptable to the Government of the Union of East European Soviet Republics, and must be revised very considerably.

I have the honor, etc., etc.,
    Vladmir N. Dzhoubinsky

✳ ✳ ✳

Coded radiogram, Dzhoubinsky to Krylenkoff:

25 OCTOBER, 1984
    ASCERTAIN IMMEDIATELY CAUSE OF RELEASE OF NUCLEAR ENERGY VICINITY OF NOVA ZEMBLA THIS AM
                    DZHOUBINSKY

✳ ✳ ✳

Coded radiogram, Wu Fung Tung to Sing Yat:

25 OCTOBER, 1984
    ASCERTAIN IMMEDIATELY CAUSE OF RE-

LEASE OF NUCLEAR ENERGY VICINITY OF NOVA
ZEMBLA THIS AM

WU

* * *

Letter from the Ameer of Afghanistan to UEESR Premier-President Mouzorgin and UPREA President Sung
Li-Yin:

26 October, 1984

SHERE ALI ABDALLAH, Ameer of Afghanistan,
Master of Kabul, Lord of Herat and Kandahar, Keeper of
Khyber Pass, Defender of the True Faith, Servant of the
Most High and Sword-Hand of the Prophet; Ph.D.
(Princeton); Sc.B. (Massachusetts Institute of Techno-
logy); M.A. (Oxford): to their Excellencies A.A. Mou-
zorgin, Premier-President of the Union of East European
Soviet Republics, and Sung Li-Yin, President of the
United Peoples' Republics of East Asia,

Greetings, in the name of Allah!

For the past five years, I have watched, with growing
concern, the increasing tensions between your Excellencies' respective Governments, allegedly arising out of the
so-called Khakum River question. It is my conviction that
this Khakum River dispute is the utterly fraudulent device
by which both Governments hope to create a pretext for
the invasion of India, each ostensibly to rescue that un-
happy country from the rapacity of the other. Your Excellencies must surely realize that this is a contingency
which the Government of the Kingdom of Afghanistan
cannot and will not permit; it would mean nothing short
of the national extinction of the Kingdom of Afghanistan,
and the enslavement of the Afghan people.

Your Excellencies will recall that I discussed this
matter most urgently on the occasions of my visits to your
respective capitals of Moscow and Nanking, and your
respective attitudes, on those occasions, has firmly con-

vinced me that neither of your Excellencies is by nature capable of adopting a rational or civilized attitude toward this question. It appears that neither of your Excellencies has any intention of abandoning your present war of mutual threats and blackmail until forced to do so by some overt act on the part of one or the other of your Excellencies' Governments, which would result in physical war of pan-Asiatic scope and magnitude. I am further convinced that this deplorable situation arises out of the megalomaniac ambitions of the Federal Governments of the UEESR and the UPREA, respectively, and that the different peoples of what you unblushingly call your "autonomous" republics have no ambitions except, on a rapidly diminishing order of probability, to live out their natural span of years in peace. Therefore:

In the name of ALLAH, the Merciful, the Compassionate: We, Shere Ali Abdallah, Ameer of Afghanistan, etc., do decree and command that the political entities known as the Union of East European Soviet Republics and the United Peoples' Republics of East Asia respectively are herewith abolished and dissolved into their constituent autonomous republics, each one of which shall hereafter enjoy complete sovereignty within its own borders as is right and proper.

Now, in case either of you gentlemen feel inclined to laugh this off, let me remind you of the series of mysterious disappearances of some of the most noted scientists of both the UEESR and the UPREA, and let me advise your Excellencies that these scientists are now residents and subjects of the Kingdom of Afghanistan, and are here engaged in research and development work for my Government. These gentlemen were not abducted, as you gentlemen seem to believe; they came here of their own free will, and ask nothing better than to remain here, where they are treated with dignity and honor, given material rewards—riches, palaces, harems, retinues of servants, etc.—and are also free from the intellectual and ideological restraints which make life so intolerable in your respective countries to any man above the order of intelligence of a cretin. In return for these benefactions, these eminent scientists have developed, for my Government, certain weapons. For example:

1.) A nuclear-rocket guided missile, officially designated as the Sword of Islam, vastly superior to your Excellencies' respective guided missiles Marxist Victory and Celestial Destroyer. It should be; it was the product of the joint efforts of Dr. Voronoff and Dr. Bao Hu-Shin, whom your Excellencies know.

2.) A new type of radar-radio-electronic defense screen, which can not only detect the approach of a guided missile, at any velocity whatever, but will automatically capture and redirect same. In case either of your Excellencies doubt this statement, you are invited to aim a rocket at some target in Afghanistan and see what happens.

3.) Both the UPREA mutated virus and the UEESR contagious sterility, with positive vaccines against the former and means of instrumental detection of the latter.

4.) A technique for initiating and controlling the Bethe carbon-hydrogen cycle. We are now using this as a source of heat for industrial and even domestic purposes, and we also have a carbon-hydrogen cycle bomb. Such a bomb, delivered by one of our Sword of Islam Mark IV's, was activated yesterday over the Northern tip of Nova Zembla, at an altitude of four miles. I am enclosing photographic reproductions of views of this test, televised to Kabul by an accompanying Sword of Islam Mark V observation rocket. I am informed that expeditions have been sent by both the UEESR and the UPREA to investigate; they should find some very interesting conditions. For one thing, they won't need their climbing equipment to get over the Nova Zembla Glacier; the Nova Zembla Glacier isn't there, any more.

5.) A lithium bomb. This has not been tested, yet. A lithium bomb is nothing for a country the size of Afghanistan to let off inside its own borders. We intend making a test with it within the next ten days, however If your Excellencies will designate a target, which must be at the center of an uninhabited area at least five hundred miles square, the test can be made in perfect safety. If not, I cannot answer the results; that will be in the hands of Allah, Who has ordained all things. No doubt Allah has ordained the destruction of either Moscow or Nanking; whichever city Allah has elected to erase, I will make it my personal responsibility to see to it that the other isn't slighted, either.

However, if your Excellencies decide to accede to my modest and reasonable demands, not later than one week from today, this test-launching will be cancelled as unnecessary. Of course, that would leave unsettled a bet I have made with Dr. Hong Foo—a star sapphire against his favorite Persian concubine—that the explosion of a lithium bomb will not initiate a chain reaction in the Earth's crust and so disintegrate this planet. This, of course, is a minor consideration, unworthy of Your notice.

Of course, I am aware that both your Excellencies have, in the past, fomented mutual jealousies and suspicions among the several "autonomous" republics under your respective jurisdictions, as an instrument of policy. If these peoples were, at this time, to receive full independence, the present inevitability of a pan-Asiatic war on a grand scale would be replaced only by the inevitability of a pan-Asiatic war by detail. Obviously, some single supra-national sovereignty is needed to maintain peace, and such a sovereignty should be established under some leadership not hitherto associated with either the former UEESR or the former UPREA. I humbly offer myself as President of such a supra-national organization, counting as a matter of course upon the wholehearted support and co-operation of both your Excellencies. It might be well if both your Excellencies were to come here to Kabul to confer with me on this subject at your very earliest convenience.

The Peace of Allah be upon both your Excellencies!
Shere Ali Abdallah, Ph.D., Sc.B., M.A.

*   *   *

From *N. Y. Times*, Oct. 30, 1984:
MOUZORGIN, SUN LI-YIN,
FÊTED AT KABUL
Confer With Ameer;
Discuss Peace Plans
Surprise Developments Seen. . . .

THE ANSWER

For a moment, after the screen door snapped and wakened him, Lee Richardson sat breathless and motionless, his eyes still closed, trying desperately to cling to the dream and print it upon his conscious memory before it faded.

"Are you there, Lee?" he heard Alexis Pitov's voice.

"Yes, I'm here. What time is it?" he asked, and then added, "I fell asleep. I was dreaming."

It was all right; he was going to be able to remember. He could still see the slim woman with the graying blonde hair, playing with the little dachshund among the new-fallen leaves on the lawn. He was glad they'd both been in this dream together; these dream-glimpses were all he'd had for the last fifteen years, and they were too precious to lose. He opened his eyes. The Russian was sitting just outside the light from the open door of the bungalow, lighting a cigarette. For a moment, he could see the blocky, high-cheeked face, now pouched and wrinkled, and then the flame went out and there was only the red coal glowing in the darkness. He closed his eyes again, and the dream picture came back to him, the woman catching the little dog and raising her head as though to speak to him.

"Plenty of time, yet." Pitov was speaking German instead of Spanish, as they always did between themselves. "They're still counting down from minus three hours. I just phoned the launching site for a jeep. Eugenio's been there ever since dinner; they say he's running around like a cat looking for a place to have her first litter of kittens."

He chuckled. This would be something new for

Eugenio Galvez — for which he could be thankful.

"I hope the generators don't develop any last-second bugs," he said. "We'll only be a mile and a half away, and that'll be too close to fifty kilos of negamatter if the field collapses."

"It'll be all right," Pitov assured him. "The bugs have all been chased out years ago."

"Not out of those generators in the rocket. They're new." He fumbled in his coat pocket for his pipe and tobacco. "I never thought I'd run another nuclear-bomb test, as long as I lived."

"Lee!" Pitov was shocked. "You mustn't call it that. It isn't that, at all. It's purely a scientific experiment."

"Wasn't that all any of them were? We made lots of experiments like this, back before 1969." The memories of all those other tests, each ending in an Everest-high mushroom column, rose in his mind. And the end result — the United States and the Soviet Union blasted to rubble, a whole hemisphere pushed back into the Dark Ages, a quarter of a billion dead. Including a slim woman with graying blonde hair, and a little red dog, and a girl from Odessa whom Alexis Pitov had been going to marry. "Forgive me, Alexis. I just couldn't help remembering. I suppose it's this shot we're going to make, tonight. It's so much like the other ones, before —" He hesitated slightly. "Before the Auburn Bomb."

There; he'd come out and said it. In all the years they'd worked together at the *Instituto Argentino de Ciencia Fisica*, that had been unmentioned between them. The families of hanged cutthroats avoid mention of ropes and knives. He thumbed the old-fashioned American lighter and held it to his pipe. Across the veranda, in the darkness, he knew that Pitov was looking intently at him.

"You've been thinking about that, lately, haven't you?" the Russian asked, and then, timidly: "Was that what you were dreaming of?"

"Oh, no, thank heaven!"

"I think about it, too, always. I suppose —" He seemed relieved, now that it had been brought out into the open and could be discussed. "You saw it fall, didn't you?"

"That's right. From about thirty miles away. A little closer than we'll be to this shot, tonight. I was in charge of the investigation at Auburn, until we had New York and Washington and Detroit and Mobile and San Francisco to worry about. Then what had happened to Auburn wasn't important, any more. We were trying to get evidence to lay before the United Nations. We kept at it for about twelve hours after the United Nations had ceased to exist."

"I could never understand about that, Lee. I don't know what the truth is; I probably never shall. But I know that my government did not launch that missile. During the first days after yours began coming in, I talked to people who had been in the Kremlin at the time. One had been in the presence of Klyzenko himself when the news of your bombardment arrived. He said that Klyzenko was absolutely stunned. We always believed that your government decided upon a preventive surprise attack, and picked out a town, Auburn, New York, that had been hit by one of our first retaliation missiles, and claimed that it had been hit first."

He shook his head. "Auburn was hit an hour before the first American missile was launched. I know that to be a fact. We could never understand why you launched just that one, and no more until after ours began landing on you; why you threw away the advantage of surprise and priority of attack —"

"Because we didn't do it, Lee!" The Russian's voice trembled with earnestness. "You believe me when I tell you that?"

"Yes, I believe you. After all that happened, and all that you, and I, and the people you worked with, and the people I worked with, and your government, and mine, have been guilty of, it would be a waste of breath for either of us to try to lie to the other about what happened fifteen years ago." He drew slowly on his pipe. "But who launched it, then? It had to be launched by somebody."

"Don't you think I've been tormenting myself with that question for the last fifteen years?" Pitov demanded. "You know, there were people inside the Soviet Union — not many, and they kept themselves well hidden — who were dedicated to the overthrow of the Soviet regime. They, or some of them, might have thought that the devastation of both our countries, and the obliteration of civilization in the Northern Hemisphere, would be a cheap price to pay for ending the rule of the Communist Party."

"Could they have built an ICBM with a thermonuclear warhead in secret?" he asked. "There were also fanatical nationalist groups in Europe, both sides of the Iron Curtain, who might have thought our mutual destruction would be worth the risks involved."

"There was China, and India. If your country and mine wiped each other out, they could go back to the old ways and the old traditions. Or Japan, or the Moslem States. In the end, they all went down along with us, but what criminal ever expects to fall?"

"We have too many suspects, and the trail's too cold, Alexis. That rocket wouldn't have had to have been launched anywhere in the Northern Hemisphere. For instance, our friends here in the Argentine have been doing very well by themselves since *El Coloso del Norte* went down."

And there were the Australians, picking themselves up bargains in real-estate in the East Indies at gun-point, and there were the Boers, trekking north again, in tanks instead of ox-wagons. And Brazil, with a not-too-implausible pretender to the Braganza throne, calling itself the Portuguese Empire and looking eastward. And, to complete the picture, here were Professor Doctor Lee Richardson and Comrade Professor Alexis Petrovitch Pitov, getting ready to test a missile with a matter-annihilation warhead.

No. This thing just wasn't a weapon.

A jeep came around the corner, lighting the dark roadway between the bungalows, its radio on and counting down — *Twenty two minutes. Twenty one fifty nine, fifty eight, fifty seven* — It came to a stop in front of their bungalow, at exactly Minus Two Hours, Twenty One Minutes, Fifty Four Seconds. The driver called out in Spanish:

"Doctor Richardson; Doctor Pitov! Are you ready?"

"Yes, ready. We're coming."

They both got to their feet, Richardson pulling himself up reluctantly. The older you get, the harder it is to leave a comfortable chair. He settled himself beside his colleague and former enemy, and the jeep started again, rolling between the buildings of the living-quarters area and out onto the long, straight road across the pampas toward the distant blaze of electric lights.

He wondered why he had been thinking so much, lately, about the Auburn Bomb. He'd questioned, at times, indignantly, of course, whether Russia had launched it — but it wasn't until tonight, until he had heard what Pitov had had to say, that he seriously doubted it. Pitov wouldn't lie about it, and Pitov would have been in a position to have known the truth, if the missile had been launched from Russia. Then he stopped thinking about what was water — or blood — a long time over the dam.

The special policeman at the entrance to the launching site reminded them that they were both smoking; when they extinguished, respectively, their cigarette and pipe, he waved the jeep on and went back to his argument with a carload of tourists who wanted to get a good view of the launching.

"There, now, Lee; do you need anything else to convince you that this isn't a weapon project?" Pitov asked.

"No, now that you mention it. I don't. You know, I

don't believe I've had to show an identity card the whole time I've been here."

"I don't believe I have an identity card," Pitov said. "Think of that."

The lights blazed everywhere around them, but mostly about the rocket that towered above everything else, so thick that it seemed squat. The gantry-cranes had been hauled away, now, and it stood alone, but it was still wreathed in thick electric cables. They were pouring enough current into that thing to light half the street-lights in Buenos Aires; when the cables were blown free by separation charges at the blastoff, the generators pow-ered by the rocket-engines had better be able to take over, because if the magnetic field collapsed and that fifty-kilo chunk of negative-proton matter came in contact with natural positive-proton matter, an old-fashioned H-bomb would be a firecracker to what would happen. Just one hundred kilos of pure, two-hundred proof MC2.

The driver took them around the rocket, dodging assorted trucks and mobile machinery that were being hurried out of the way. The countdown was just beyond two hours five minutes. The jeep stopped at the edge of a crowd around three more trucks, and Doctor Eugenio Galvez, the director of the Institute, left the crowd and approached at an awkward half-run as they got down.

"Is everything checked, gentlemen?" he wanted to know.

"It was this afternoon at 1730," Pitov told him. "And nobody's been burning my telephone to report anything different. Are the balloons and the drone planes ready?"

"The Air Force just finished checking; they're ready. Captain Urquiola flew one of the planes over the course and made a guidance-tape; that's been duplicated and all the planes are equipped with copies."

"How's the wind?" Richardson asked.

"Still steady. We won't have any trouble about fallout or with the balloons."

"Then we'd better go back to the bunker and make sure everybody there is on the job."

The loudspeaker was counting down to Two Hours One Minute.

"Could you spare a few minutes to talk to the press?" Eugenio Galvez asked. "And perhaps say a few words for telecast? This last is most important; we can't explain too many times the purpose of this experiment. There is still much hostility, arising from fear that we are testing a nuclear weapon."

The press and telecast services were well represented; there were close to a hundred correspondents, from all over South America, from South Africa and Australia, even one from Ceylon. They had three trucks, with mobile telecast pickups, and when they saw who was approaching, they released the two rocketry experts they had been quizzing and pounced on the new victims.

Was there any possibility that negative-proton matter might be used as a weapon?

"Anything can be used as a weapon; you could stab a man to death with that lead pencil you're using," Pitov replied. "But I doubt if negamatter will ever be so used. We're certainly not working on weapons design here. We started, six years ago, with the ability to produce negative protons, reverse-spin neutrons, and positrons, and the theoretical possibility of assembling them into negamatter. We have just gotten a fifty kilogramme mass of nega-iron assembled. In those six years, we had to invent all our techniques, and design all our equipment. If we'd been insane enough to want to build a nuclear weapon, after what we went through up North, we could have done so from memory, and designed a better — which is to say a worse—one from memory in a few days."

"Yes, and building a negamatter bomb for military purposes would be like digging a fifty foot shaft to get a rock to bash somebody's head in, when you could do the job better with the shovel you're digging with," Richardson added. "The time, money, energy and work we put in on this thing would be ample to construct twenty thermonuclear bombs. And that's only a small part of it." He went on to tell them about the magnetic bottle inside the rocket's warhead, mentioning how much electric current was needed to keep up the magnetic field that insulated the negamatter from contact with posimatter.

"Then what was the purpose of this experiment, Doctor Richardson?"

"Oh, we were just trying to find out a few basic facts about natural structure. Long ago, it was realized that the nucleonic particles — protons, neutrons, mesons and so on — must have structure of their own. Since we started constructing negative-proton matter, we've found out a few things about nucleonic structure. Some rather odd things, including fractions of Planck's constant."

A couple of the correspondents — a man from La Prensa, and an Australian — whistled softly. The others looked blank. Pitov took over:

"You see, gentlemen, most of what we learned, we learned from putting negamatter atoms together. We annihilated a few of them — over there in that little concrete building, we have one of the most massive steel vaults in the world, where we do that — but we assembled millions of them for every one we annihilated, and that chunk of nega-iron inside the magnetic bottle kept growing. And when you have a piece of negamatter you don't want, you can't just throw it out on the scrap-pile. We might have rocketed it into escape velocity and let it blow up in space, away from the Moon or any of the artificial satellites, but why waste it? So we're going to have the rocket eject it, and when it falls, we can see, by our telemetered instruments, just what happens."

"Well, won't it be annihilated by contact with atmosphere?" somebody asked.

"That's one of the things we want to find out," Pitov said. "We estimate about twenty percent loss from contact with atmosphere, but the mass that actually lands on the target area should be about forty kilos. It should be something of a spectacle, coming down."

"You say you had to assemble it, after creating the negative protons and neutrons and the positrons. Doesn't any of this sort of matter exist in nature?"

The man who asked that knew better himself. He just wanted the answer on the record.

"Oh no; not on this planet, and probably not in the Galaxy. There may be whole galaxies composed of nothing but negamatter. There may even be isolated stars and planetary systems inside our Galaxy composed of negamatter, though I think that very improbable. But when negamatter and posimatter come into contact with one another, the result is immediate mutual annihilation."

They managed to get away from the press, and returned as far as the bunkers, a mile and a half away. Before they went inside, Richardson glanced up at the sky, fixing the location of a few of the more conspicuous stars in his mind. There were almost a hundred men and women inside, each at his or her instruments — view-screens, radar indicators, detection instruments of a dozen kinds. The reporters and telecast people arrived shortly afterward, and Eugenio Galvez took them in tow. While Richardson and Pitov were making their last-minute rounds, the countdown progressed past minus one hour, and at minus twenty minutes all the overhead lights went off and the small instrument operators' lights came on.

Pitov turned on a couple of view-screens, one from a pickup on the roof of the bunker and another from the launching-pad. They sat down side by side and waited. Richardson got his pipe out and began loading it. The loudspeaker was saying: *"Minus two minutes, one fifty nine, fifty eight, fifty seven —"*

He let his mind drift away from the test, back to the world that had been smashed around his ears in the autumn of 1969. He was doing that so often, now, when he should be thinking about —

"*Two seconds, one second.* FIRING!"

It was a second later that his eyes focussed on the left hand view-screen. Red and yellow flames were gushing out at the bottom of the rocket, and it was beginning to tremble. Then the upper jets, the ones that furnished power for the generators, began firing. He looked anxiously at the meters; the generators were building up power. Finally, when he was sure that the rocket would be blasting off anyhow, the separator-charges fired and the heavy cables fell away. An instant later, the big missile started inching upward, gaining speed by the second, first slowly and jerkily and then more rapidly, until it passed out of the field of the pickup. He watched the rising spout of fire from the other screen until it passed from sight.

By that time, Pitov had twisted a dial and gotten another view on the left hand screen, this time from close to the target. That camera was radar-controlled; it had fastened onto the approaching missile, which was still invisible. The stars swung slowly across the screen until Richardson recognized the ones he had spotted at the zenith. In a moment, now, the rocket, a hundred miles overhead, would be nosing down, and then the warhead would open and the magnetic field inside would alter and the mass of negamatter would be ejected.

The stars were blotted out by a sudden glow of light. Even at a hundred miles, there was enough atmospheric density to produce considerable energy release. Pitov, beside him, was muttering, partly in German and partly in Russian; most of what Richardson caught was figures. Trying to calculate how much of the mass of unnatural iron would get down for the ground blast. Then the right hand screen broke into a wriggling orgy of color, and at the same time every scrap of radio-transmitted apparatus either went out or began reporting erratically. The left hand screen, connected by wiring to the pickup on the roof, was still functioning. For a moment, Richardson wondered what was going on, and then shocked recognition drove that from his mind as he stared at the ever-brightening glare in the sky.

It was the Auburn Bomb again! He was back, in memory, to the night on the shore of Lake Ontario; the party breaking up in the early hours of morning; he and Janet and the people with whom they had been spending a vacation week standing on the lawn as the guests were getting into their cars. And then the sudden light in the sky. The cries of surprise, and then of alarm as it seemed to be rushing straight down upon them. He and Janet, clutching each other and staring up in terror at the falling blaze from which there seemed no escape. Then relief, as it curved away from them and fell to the south. And then the explosion, lighting the whole southern sky.

There was a similar explosion in the screen, when the mass of nega-iron landed — a sheet of pure white light, so bright and so quick as to almost pass above the limit of visibility, and then a moment's darkness that was in his stunned eyes more than in the screen, and then the rising glow of updrawn incandescent dust.

Before the sound-waves had reached them, he had been legging it into the house. The television had been on, and it had been acting as insanely as the screen on his right now. He had called the State Police — the telephones had been working all right — and told them who he was, and they had told him to stay put and they'd send a car for him. They did, within minutes. Janet and his host and hostess had waited with him on the lawn until it came, and after he had gotten into it, he had turned around and looked back through the rear window, and seen Janet standing under the front light, holding the little dog in her arms, flopping one of its silly little paws up and down with her hand to wave goodbye to him.

He had seen her and the dog like that every day of his life for the last fifteen years.

"What kind of radiation are you getting?" he could hear Alexis Pitov asking into a phone. "What? Nothing else? Oh; yes, of course. But mostly cosmic. That shouldn't last long." He turned from the phone. "A devil's own dose of cosmic, and some gamma. It was the cosmic radiation that put the radios and telescreens out. That's why I insisted that the drone planes be independent of radio control."

They always got cosmic radiation from the micro-annihilations in the test-vault. Well, now they had an idea of what produced natural cosmic rays. There must be quite a bit of negamatter and posimatter going into mutual annihilation and total energy release through the Universe.

"Of course, there were no detectors set up in advance around Auburn," he said. "We didn't really begin to find anything out for half an hour. By that time, the cosmic radiation was over and we weren't getting anything but gamma."

"What — What has Auburn to do — ?" The Russian stopped short. "You think this was the same thing?" He gave it a moment's consideration. "Lee, you're crazy! There wasn't an atom of artificial negamatter in the world in 1969. Nobody had made any before us. We gave each other some scientific surprises, then, but nobody surprised both of us. You and I, between us, knew everything that was going on in nuclear physics in the world. And you know as well as I do —"

A voice came out of the public-address speaker. "Some of the radio equipment around the target area, that wasn't knocked out by blast, is beginning to function again. There is an increasingly heavy gamma radiation, but no more cosmic rays. They were all prompt radiation from the annihilation; the gamma is secondary effect. Wait a moment; Captain Urquiola, of the Air Force, says that the first drone plane is about to take off."

It had been two hours after the blast that the first

drones had gone over what had been Auburn, New York. He was trying to remember, as exactly as possible, what had been learned from them. Gamma radiation; a great deal of gamma. But it didn't last long. It had been almost down to a safe level by the time the investigation had been called off, and, two months after there had been no more missiles, and no way of producing more, and no targets to send them against if they'd had them, rather — he had been back at Auburn on his hopeless quest, and there had been almost no trace of radiation. Nothing but a wide, shallow crater, almost two hundred feet in diameter and only fifteen at its deepest, already full of water, and a circle of flattened and scattered rubble for a mile and a half all around it. He was willing to bet anything that that was what they'd find where the chunk of nega-iron had landed, fifty miles away on the pampas.

Well, the first drone ought to be over the target area before long, and at least one of the balloons that had been sent up was reporting its course by radio. The radios in the others were silent, and the recording counters had probably jammed in all of them. There'd be something of interest when the first drone came back. He dragged his mind back to the present, and went to work with Alexis Pitov.

They were at it all night, checking, evaluating, making sure that the masses of data that were coming in were being promptly processed for programming the computers. At each of the increasingly frequent coffee-breaks, he noticed Pitov looking curiously. He said nothing, however, until, long after dawn, they stood outside the bunker, waiting for the jeep that would take them back to their bungalow and watching the line of trucks — Argentine army engineers, locally hired laborers, load after load of prefab-huts and equipment — going down toward the target-area, where they would be working for the next week.

"Lee, were you serious?" Pitov asked. "I mean, about

this being like the one at Auburn?"

"It was exactly like Auburn; even that blazing light that came rushing down out of the sky. I wondered about that at the time — what kind of a missile would produce an effect like that. Now I know. We just launched one like it."

"But that's impossible! I told you, between us we know everything that was happening in nuclear physics then. Nobody in the world knew how to assemble atoms of negamatter and build them into masses."

"Nobody, and nothing, on this planet built that mass of negamatter. I doubt if it even came from this Galaxy. But we didn't know that, then. When that negamatter meteor fell, the only thing anybody could think of was that it had been a Soviet missile. If it had hit around Leningrad or Moscow or Kharkov, who would you have blamed it on?"

LAST ENEMY

Along the U-shaped table, the subdued clatter of dinnerware and the buzz of conversation was dying out; the soft music that drifted down from the overhead sound outlets seemed louder as the competing noises diminished. The feast was drawing to a close, and Dallona of Hadron fidgeted nervously with the stem of her wineglass as last-moment doubts assailed her.

The old man at whose right she sat noticed, and reached out to lay his hand on hers.

"My dear, you're worried," he said softly. "You, of all people, shouldn't be, you know."

"The theory isn't complete," she replied. "And I could wish for more positive verification. I'd hate to think I'd got you into this—"

Garnon of Roxor laughed. "No, no!" he assured her. "I'd decided upon this long before you announced the results of your experiments. Ask Girzon; he'll bear me out."

"That's true," the young man who sat at Garnon's left said, leaning forward. "Father has meant to take this step for a long time. He was waiting until after the election, and then he decided to do it now, to give you an opportunity to make experimental use of it."

The man on Dallona's right added his voice. Like the others at the table, he was of medium stature, brown-skinned and dark-eyed, with a wide mouth, prominent cheekbones and a short, square jaw. Unlike the others, he was armed, with a knife and pistol on his belt, and on the breast of his black tunic he wore a scarlet oval patch on which a pair of black wings, with a tapering silver object between them had been superimposed.

"Yes, Lady Dallona; the Lord Garnon and I discussed this, oh, two years ago at the least. Really, I'm surprised that you seem to shrink from it, now. Of course, you're Venus-born, and customs there may be different, but with your scientific knowledge—"

"That may be the trouble, Dirzed," Dallona told him. "A scientist gets in the way of doubting, and one doubts one's own theories most of all."

"That's the scientific attitude, I'm told," Dirzed replied, smiling. "But somehow, I cannot think of you as a scientist." His eyes traveled over her in a way that would have made most women, scientists or otherwise, blush. It gave Dallona of Hadron a feeling of pleasure. Men often looked at her that way, especially here at Darsh. Novelty had something to do with it—her skin was considerably lighter than usual, and there was a pleasing oddness about the structure of her face. Her alleged Venusian origin was probably accepted as the explanation of that, as of so many other things.

As she was about to reply, a man in dark gray, one of the upper-servants who were accepted as social equals by the Akor-Neb nobles, approached the table. He nodded respectfully to Garnon of Roxor.

"I hate to seem to hurry things, sir, but the boy's ready. He's in a trance-state now," he reported, pointing to the pair of visiplates at the end of the room.

Both of the ten-foot-square plates were activated. One was a solid luminous white; on the other was the image of a boy of twelve or fourteen, seated at a big writing machine. Even allowing for the fact that the boy was in a hypnotic trance, there was an expression of idiocy on his loose-lipped, slack-jawed face, a pervading dullness.

"One of our best sensitives," a man with a beard, several places down the table on Dallona's right, said. "You remember him, Dallona; he produced that communication from the discarnate Assassin, Sirzim. Normally, he's a low-grade imbecile, but in trance-state he's wonderful. And there can be no argument that the communications he produces originates in his own mind; he doesn't have mind enough, of his own, to operate that machine."

Garnon of Roxor rose to his feet, the others rising with him. He unfastened a jewel from the front of his tunic and handed it to Dallona.

"Here, my dear Lady Dallona; I want you to have this," he said. "It's been in the family of Roxor for six generations, but I know that you will appreciate and cherish it." He twisted a heavy ring from his left hand and gave it to his son. He unstrapped his wrist watch and passed it across the table to the gray-clad upper-servant. He gave a pocket case, containing writing tools, slide rule and magnifier, to the bearded man on the other side of Dallona. "Something you can use, Dr. Harnosh," he said. Then he took a belt, with a knife and holstered pistol, from a servant who had brought it to him, and gave it to the man with the red badge. "And something for you, Dirzed. The pistol's by Farnor of Yand, and the knife was forged and tempered on Luna."

The man with the winged-bullet badge took the weapons, exclaiming in appreciation. Then he removed his own belt and buckled on the gift.

"The pistol's fully loaded," Garnon told him.

Dirzed drew it and checked—a man of his craft took no statement about weapons without verification—then slipped it back into the holster.

"Shall I use it?" he asked.

"By all means; I'd had that in mind when I selected it for you."

Another man, to the left of Girzon, received a cigarette case and lighter. He and Garnon hooked fingers and clapped shoulders.

"Our views haven't been the same, Garnon," he said, "but I've always valued your friendship. I'm sorry you're doing this, now; I believe you'll be disappointed."

Garnon chuckled. "Would you care to make a small wager on that, Nirzav?" he asked. "You know what I'm putting up. If I'm proven right, will you accept the Volitionalist theory as verified?"

Nirzav chewed his mustache for a moment. "Yes, Garnon, I will." He pointed toward the blankly white screen. "If we get anything conclusive on that, I'll have no other choice."

"All right, friends," Garnon said to those around him. "Will you walk with me to the end of the room?"

Servants removed a section from the table in front of him, to allow him and a few others to pass through; the rest of the guests remained standing at the table, facing toward the inside of the room. Garnon's son, Girzon, and the gray-mustached Nirzav of Shonna, walked on his left; Dallona of Hadron and Dr. Harnosh of Hosh on his right. The gray-clad upper-servant, and two or three ladies, and a nobleman with a small chin-beard, and several others, joined them; of those who had sat close to Garnon, only the man in the black tunic with the scarlet badge hung back. He stood still, by the break in the table, watching Garnon of Roxor walk away from him. Then Dirzed the Assassin drew the pistol he had lately received as a gift, hefted it in his hand, thumbed off the safety, and aimed at the back of Garnon's head.

They had nearly reached the end of the room when the pistol cracked. Dallona of Hadron started, almost as though the bullet had crashed into her own body, then caught herself and kept on walking. She closed her eyes and laid a hand on Dr. Harnosh's arm for guidance, concentrating her mind upon a single question. The others went on as though Garnon of Roxor were still walking among them.

"Look!" Harnosh of Hosh cried, pointing to the image in the visiplate ahead. "He's under control!"

They all stopped short, and Dirzed, holstering his pistol, hurried forward to join them. Behind, a couple of servants had approached with a stretcher and were gathering up the crumpled figure that had, a moment ago, been Garnon.

A change had come over the boy at the writing machine. His eyes were still glazed with the stupor of the hypnotic trance, but the slack jaw had stiffened, and the loose mouth was compressed in a purposeful line. As they watched, his hands went out to the keyboard in front of him and began to move over it, and as they did, letters appeared on the white screen on the left.

Garnon of Roxor, discarnate, communicating, they read. The machine stopped for a moment, then began again. *To Dallona of Hadron: The question you asked, after I discarnated, was: What was the last book I read, before the feast? While waiting for my valet to prepare my bath, I read the first ten verses of the fourth Canto of "Splendor of Space," by Larnov of Horka, in my bedroom. When the bath was ready, I marked the page with a strip of message tape, containing a message from the bailiff of my estate on the Shevva River, concerning a breakdown at the power plant, and laid the book on the ivory-inlaid table beside the big red chair.*

Harnosh of Hosh looked at Dallona inquiringly; she nodded.

"I rejected the question I had in my mind, and substituted that one, after the shot," she said.

He turned quickly to the upper-servant. "Check on that, right away, Kirzon," he directed.

As the upper-servant hurried out, the writing machine started again.

And to my son, Girzon: I will not use your son, Garnon, as a reincarnation-vehicle; I will remain discarnate until he is grown and has a son of his own; if he has no male child, I will reincarnate in the first available male child of the family of Roxor, or of some family allied to us by marriage. In any case, I will communicate before reincarnating.

To Nirzav of Shonna: Ten days ago, when I dined at your home, I took a small knife and cut three notches, two close together and one a little apart from the others, on the under side of the table. As I remember, I sat two places down on the left. If you find them, you will know that I have won that wager that I spoke of a few minutes ago.

"I'll have my butler check on that, right away," Nirzav said. His eyes were wide with amazement, and he had begun to sweat; a man does not casually watch the beliefs of a lifetime invalidated in a few moments.

To Dirzed the Assassin: the machine continued. *You have served me faithfully, in the last ten years, never more so than with the last shot you fired in my service. After you fired, the thought was in your mind that you would like to take service with the Lady Dallona of Hadron, whom you believe will need the protection of a member of the Society of Assassins. I advise you to do so, and I advise her to accept your offer. Her work, since she has come to Darsh, has not made her popular in some quarters. No doubt Nirzav of Shonna can bear me out on that.*

"I won't betray things told me in confidence, or said at the Councils of the Statisticalists, but he's right," Nirzav said. "You need a good Assassin, and there are few better than Dirzed."

I see that this sensitive is growing weary, the letters on the screen spelled out. *His body is not strong enough for prolonged communication. I bid you all farewell, for the time; I will communicate again. Good evening, my friends, and I thank you for your presence at the feast.*

The boy, on the other screen, slumped back in his chair, his face relaxing into its customary expression of vacancy.

"Will you accept my offer of service, Lady Dallona?" Dirzed asked. "It's as Garnon said; you've made enemies."

Dallona smiled at him. "I've not been too deep in my work to know that. I'm glad to accept your offer, Dirzed."

Nirzav of Shonna had already turned away from the group and was hurrying from the room, to call his home for confirmation on the notches made on the underside of his dining table. As he went out the door, he almost collided with the upper-servant, who was rushing in with a book in his hand.

"Here it is," the latter exclaimed, holding up the book. "Larnov's 'Splendor of Space,' just where he said it would be. I had a couple of servants with me as witnesses; I can call them in now, if you wish." He handed the book to Harnosh of Hosh. "See, a strip of message tape in it, at the tenth verse of the Fourth Canto."

Nirzav of Shonna re-entered the room; he was chewing his mustache and muttering to himself. As he rejoined the group in front of the now dark visiplates, he raised his voice, addressing them all generally.

"My butler found the notches, just as the communication described," he said. "This settles it! Garnon, if you're where you can hear me, you've won. I can't believe in the Statisticalist doctrines after this, or in the political program based upon them. I'll announce my change of attitude at the next meeting of the Executive Council, and resign my seat. I was elected by Statisticalist votes, and I cannot hold office as a Volitionalist."

"You'll need a couple of Assassins, too," the nobleman with the chin-beard told him. "Your former colleagues and fellow-party-members are regrettably given to the forcible discarnation of those who differ with them."

"I've never employed personal Assassins before," Nirzav replied, "but I think you're right. As soon as I get home, I'll call Assassins' Hall and make the necessary arrangements."

"Better do it now," Girzon of Roxor told him, lowering his voice. "There are over a hundred guests here, and I can't vouch for all of them. The Statisticalists would be sure to have a spy planted among them. My father was one of their most dangerous opponents, when he was on the Council; they've always been afraid he'd come out of retirement and stand for re-election. They'd want to make sure he was really discarnate. And if that's the case, you can be sure your change of attitude is known to old Mirzark of Bashad by this time. He won't dare allow you to make a public renunciation of Statisticalism." He turned to the other nobleman. "Prince Jirzyn, why don't you call the Volitionist headquarters and have a couple of our Assassins sent here to escort Lord Nirzav home?"

"I'll do that immediately," Jirzyn of Starpha said. "It's as Lord Girzon says; we can be pretty sure there was a spy among the guests, and now that you've come over to our way of thinking, we're responsible for your safety."

He left the room to make the necessary visiphone call. Dallona, accompanied by Dirzed, returned to her place at the table, where she was joined by Harnosh of Hosh and some of the others.

"There's no question about the results," Harnosh was exulting. "I'll grant that the boy might have picked up some of that stuff telepathically from the carnate minds present here; even from the mind of Garnon, before he was discarnated. But he could not have picked up enough data, in that way, to make a connected and coherent communication. It takes a sensitive with a powerful mind of his own to practice telesthesia, and that boy's almost an idiot." He turned to Dallona. "You asked a question, mentally, after Garnon was discarnate, and got an answer that could have been contained only in Garnon's mind. I think it's conclusive proof that the discarnate Garnon was fully conscious and communicating."

"Dirzed also asked a question, mentally, after the discarnation, and got an answer. Dr. Harnosh, we can state positively that the surviving individuality is fully conscious in the discarnate state, is telepathically sensitive, and is capable of telepathic communication with other minds," Dallona agreed. "And in view of our earlier work with memory-recalls, we're justified in stating positively that the individual is capable of exercising choice in reincarnation vehicles."

"My father had been considering voluntary discarnation for a long time," Girzon of Roxor said. "Ever since the discarnation of my mother. He deferred that step because he was unwilling to deprive the Volitionalist Party of his support. Now it would seem that he has done more to combat Statisticalism by discarnating than he ever did in his carnate existence."

"I don't know, Girzon," Jirzyn of Starpha said, as he joined the group. "The Statisticalists will denounce the whole thing as a prearranged fraud. And if they can discarnate the Lady Dallona before she can record her testimony under truth hypnosis or on a lie detector, we're no better off than we were before. Dirzed, you have a great responsibility in guarding the Lady Dallona; some extraordinary security precautions will be needed."

In his office, in the First Level city of Dhergabar, Tortha Karf, Chief of Paratime Police, leaned forward in his chair to hold his lighter for his special assistant, Verkan Vall, then lit his own cigarette. He was a man of middle age—his three hundredth birthday was only a decade or so off—and he had begun to acquire a double chin and a bulge at his waistline. His hair, once black, had turned a uniform iron-gray and was beginning to thin in front.

"What do you know about the Second Level Akor-Neb Sector, Vall?" he inquired. "Ever work in that paratime-area?"

Verkan Vall's handsome features became even more immobile than usual as he mentally pronounced the verbal trigger symbols which should bring hypnotically-acquired knowledge into his conscious mind. Then he shook his head.

"Must be a singularly well-behaved sector, sir," he

said. "Or else we've been lucky, so far. I never was on an Akor-Neb operation; don't even have a hypno-mech for that sector. All I know is from general reading.

"Like all the Second Level, its time-lines descend from the probability of one or more shiploads of colonists having come to Terra from Mars about seventy-five to a hundred thousand years ago, and then having been cut off from the home planet and forced to develop a civilization of their own here. The Akor-Neb civilization is of a fairly high culture-order, even for Second Level. An atomic-power, interplanetary culture; gravity-counteraction, direct conversion of nuclear energy to electrical power, that sort of thing. We buy fine synthetic plastics and fabrics from them." He fingered the material of his smartly-cut green police uniform. "I think this cloth is Akor-Neb. We sell a lot of Venusian *zerfa*-leaf; they smoke it, straight and mixed with tobacco. They have a single System-wide government, a single race, and a universal language. They're a dark-brown race, which evolved in its present form about fifty thousand years ago; the present civilization is about ten thousand years old, developed out of the wreckage of several earlier civilizations which decayed or fell through wars, exhaustion of resources, et cetera. They have legends, maybe historical records, of their extraterrestrial origin."

Tortha Karf nodded. "Pretty good, for consciously acquired knowledge," he commented. "Well, our luck's run out, on that sector; we have troubles there, now. I want you to go iron them out. I know, you've been going pretty hard, lately—that nighthound business, on the Fourth Level Europo-American Sector, wasn't any picnic. But the fact is that a lot of my ordinary and deputy assistants have a little too much regard for the alleged sanctity of human life, and this is something that may need some pretty drastic action."

"Some of our people getting out of line?" Verkan Vall asked.

"Well, the data isn't too complete, but one of our people has run into trouble on that sector, and needs rescuing—a psychic-science researcher, a young lady named Hadron Dalla. I believe you know her, don't you?" Tortha Karf asked innocently.

"Slightly," Verkan Vall deadpanned. "I enjoyed a brief but rather hectic companionate-marriage with her, about twenty years ago. What sort of a jam's little Dalla got herself into, now?"

"Well, frankly, we don't know. I hope she's still alive, but I'm not unduly optimistic. It seems that about a year ago, Dr. Hadron transposed to the Second Level, to study alleged proof of reincarnation which the Akor-Neb people were reported to possess. She went to Gindrabar, on Venus, and transposed to the Second Paratime Level, to a station maintained by Outtime Import & Export Trading Corporation—a *zerfa* plantation just east of the High Ridge country. There she assumed an identity as the daughter of a planter, and took the name of Dallona of Hadron. Parenthetically, all Akor-Neb family-names are prepositional; family-names were originally place names. I believe that ancient Akor-Neb marital relations were too complicated to permit exact establishment of paternity. And all Akor-Neb men's personal names have *-irz-* or *-arn-* inserted in the middle, and women's names end in *-itra-* or *-ona*. You could call yourself Virzal of Verkan, for instance.

"Anyhow, she made the Second Level Venus-Terra trip on a regular passenger liner, and landed at the Akor-Neb city of Ghamma, on the upper Nile. There she established contact with the Outtime Trading Corporation representative, Zortan Brend, locally known as Brarnend of Zorda. He couldn't call himself Brarnend of Zortan—in the Akor-Neb language, *zortan* is a particularly nasty dirty-word. Hadron Dalla spent a few weeks at his residence, briefing herself on local conditions. Then she went to the capital city, Darsh, in eastern Europe, and enrolled as a student at something called the Independent

Institute for Reincarnation Research, having secured a letter of introduction to its director, a Dr. Harnosh of Hosh.

"Almost at once, she began sending in reports to her home organization, the Rhogom Memorial Foundation of Psychic Science, here at Dhergabar, through Zortan Brend. The people there were wildly enthusiastic. I don't have more than the average intelligent—I hope—layman's knowledge of psychics, but Dr. Volzar Darv, the director of Rhogom Foundation, tells me that even in the present incomplete form, her reports have opened whole new horizons in the science. It seems that these Akor-Neb people have actually demonstrated, as a scientific fact, that the human individuality reincarnates after physical death—that your personality, and mine, have existed, as such, for ages, and will exist for ages to come. More, they have means of recovering, from almost anybody, memories of past reincarnations.

"Well, after about a month, the people at this Reincarnation Institute realized that this Dallona of Hadron wasn't any ordinary student. She probably had trouble keeping down to the local level of psychic knowledge. So, as soon as she'd learned their techniques, she was allowed to undertake experimental work of her own. I imagine she let herself out on that; as soon as she'd mastered the standard Akor-Neb methods of recovering memories of past reincarnations, she began refining and developing them more than the local yokels had been able to do in the past thousand years. I can't tell you just what she did, because I don't know the subject, but she must have lit things up properly. She got quite a lot of local publicity; not only scientific journals, but general newscasts.

"Then, four days ago, she disappeared, and her disappearance seems to have been coincident with an unsuccessful attempt on her life. We don't know as much about this as we should; all we have is Zortan Brend's account.

"It seems that on the evening of her disappearance,

she had been attending the voluntary discarnation feast—suicide party—of a prominent nobleman named Garnon of Roxor. Evidently when the Akor-Neb people get tired of their current reincarnation they invite in their friends, throw a big party, and then do themselves in in an atmosphere of general conviviality. Frequently they take poison or inhale lethal gas; this fellow had his personal trigger man shoot him through the head. Dalla was one of the guests of honor, along with this Harnosh of Hosh. They'd made rather elaborate preparations, and after the shooting they got a detailed and apparently authentic spirit-communication from the late Garnon. The voluntary discarnation was just a routine social event, it seems, but the communication caused quite an uproar, and rated top place on the System-wide newscasts, and started a storm of controversy.

"After the shooting and the communication, Dalla took the officiating gun artist, one Dirzed, into her own service. This Dirzed was spoken of as a generally respected member of something called the Society of Assassins, and that'll give you an idea of what things are like on that sector, and why I don't want to send anybody who might develop trigger-finger cramp at the wrong moment. She and Dirzed left the home of the gentleman who had just had himself discarnated, presumably for Dalla's apartment, about a hundred miles away. That's the last that's been heard of either of them.

"This attempt on Dalla's life occurred while the premortem revels were still going on. She lived in a six-room apartment, with three servants, on one of the upper floors of a three-thousand-foot tower—Akor-Neb cities are built vertically, with considerable interval between units—and while she was at this feast, a package was delivered at the apartment, ostensibly from the Reincarnation Institute and made up to look as though it contained record tapes. One of the servants accepted it from a service employee of the apartments. The next morning, a little before noon, Dr. Harnosh of Hosh called her on the visiphone and got no answer; he then called the apartment manager, who entered the apartment. He found all three of the servants dead, from a lethal-gas bomb which had exploded when one of them had opened this package. However, Hadron Dalla had never returned to the apartment, the night before."

Verkan Vall was sitting motionless, his face expressionless as he ran Tortha Karf's narrative through the intricate semantic and psychological processes of the First Level mentality. The fact that Hadron Dalla had been a former wife of his had been relegated to one corner of his consciousness and contained there; it was not a fact that would, at the moment, contribute to the problem or to his treatment of it.

"The package was delivered while she was at this suicide party," he considered. "It must, therefore, have been sent by somebody who either did not know she would be out of the apartment, or who did not expect it to function until after her return. On the other hand, if her disappearance was due to hostile action, it was the work of somebody who knew she was at the feast and did not want her to reach her apartment again. This would seem to exclude the sender of the package bomb."

Tortha Karf nodded. He had reached that conclusion, himself.

"Thus," Verkan Vall continued, "if her disappearance was the work of an enemy, she must have two enemies, each working in ignorance of the other's plans."

"What do you think she did to provoke such enmity?"

"Well, of course, it just might be that Dalla's normally complicated love-life had got a little more complicated than usual and short-circuited on her," Verkan Vall said, out of the fullness of personal knowledge, "but I doubt that, at the moment. I would think that this affair has political implications."

"So?" Tortha Karf had not thought of politics as an explanation. He waited for Verkan Vall to elaborate.

"Don't you see, chief?" the special assistant asked. "We find a belief in reincarnation on many time-lines, as a religious doctrine, but these people accept it as a scientific fact. Such acceptance would carry much more conviction; it would influence a people's entire thinking. We see it reflected in their disregard for death—suicide as a social function, this Society of Assassins, and the like. It would naturally color their political thinking, because politics is nothing but common action to secure more favorable living conditions, and to these people, the term 'living conditions' includes not only the present life, but also an indefinite number of future lives as well. I find this title, 'Independent' Institute, suggestive. Independent of what? Possibly of partisan affiliation."

"But wouldn't these people be grateful to her for her new discoveries, which would enable them to plan their future reincarnations more intelligently?" Tortha Karf asked.

"Oh, chief!" Verkan Vall reproached. "You know better than that! How many times have our people got in trouble on other time-lines because they divulged some useful scientific fact that conflicted with the locally revered nonsense? You show me ten men who cherish some religious doctrine or political ideology, and I'll show you nine men whose minds are utterly impervious to any factual evidence which contradicts their beliefs, and who regard the producer of such evidence as a criminal who ought to be suppressed. For instance, on the Fourth Level Europo-American Sector, where I was just working, there is a political sect, the Communists, who, in the territory under their control, forbid the teaching of certain well-established facts of genetics and heredity, because those facts do not fit the world-picture demanded by their political doctrines. And on the same sector, a religious sect recently tried, in some sections successfully, to outlaw the teaching of evolution by natural selection."

Tortha Karf nodded. "I remember some stories my grandfather told me, about his narrow escapes from an organization called the Holy Inquisition, when he was a paratime trader on the Fourth Level, about four hundred years ago. I believe that thing's still operating, on the Europo-American Sector, under the name of the NKVD. So you think Dalla may have proven something that conflicted with local reincarnation theories, and somebody who had a vested interest in maintaining those theories is trying to stop her?"

"You spoke of a controversy over the communication alleged to have originated with this voluntarily discarnated nobleman. That would suggest a difference of opinion on the manner of nature of reincarnation or the discarnate state. This difference may mark the dividing line between the different political parties. Now, to get to this Darsh place, do I have to go to Venus, as Dalla did?"

"No. The Outtime Trading Corporation has transposition facilities at Ravvanan, on the Nile, which is spatially co-existent with the city of Ghamma on the Akor-Neb Sector, where Zortan Brend is. You transpose through there, and Zortan Brend will furnish you transportation to Darsh. It'll take you about two days, here, getting your hypno-mech indoctrinations and having your skin pigmented, and your hair turned black. I'll notify Zortan Brend at once that you're coming through. Is there anything special you'll want?"

"Why, I'll want an abstract of the reports Dalla sent back to Rhogom Foundation. It's likely that there is some clue among them as to whom her discoveries may have antagonized. I'm going to be a Venusian *zerfa*-planter, a friend of her father's; I'll want full hypno-mech indoctrination to enable me to play that part. And I'll want to familiarize myself with Akor-Neb weapons and combat techniques. I think that will be all, chief."

The last of the tall city-units of Ghamma were sliding out of sight as the ship passed over them—shaft-like buildings that rose two or three thousand feet above the ground in clumps of three or four or six, one at each corner of the landing stages set in series between them. Each of these units stood in the middle of a wooded park some five miles square; no unit was much more or less than twenty miles from its nearest neighbor, and the land between was the uniform golden-brown of ripening grain, crisscrossed with the threads of irrigation canals and dotted here and there with sturdy farm-village buildings and tall, stacklike granaries. There were a few other ships in the air at the fifty-thousand-foot level, and below, swarms of small airboats darted back and forth on different levels, depending upon speed and direction. Far ahead, to the northeast, was the shimmer of the Red Sea and the hazy bulk of Asia Minor beyond.

Verkan Vall—the Lord Virzal of Verkan, temporarily—stood at the glass front of the observation deck, looking down. He was a different Verkan Vall from the man who had talked with Tortha Karf in the latter's office, two days before. The First Level cosmeticists had worked miracles upon him with their art. His skin was a soft chocolate-brown, now; his hair was jet-black, and so were his eyes. And in his subconscious mind, instantly available to consciousness, was a vast body of knowledge about conditions on the Akor-Neb sector, as well as a complete command of the local language, all hypnotically acquired.

He knew that he was looking down upon one of the minor provincial cities of a very respectably advanced civilization. A civilization which built its cities vertically, since it had learned to counteract gravitation. A civilization which still depended upon natural cereals for food, but one which had learned to make the most efficient use of its soil. The network of dams and irrigation canals which he saw was as good as anything on his own paratime level. The wide dispersal of buildings, he knew, was a heritage of a series of disastrous atomic wars of several thousand years before; the Akor-Neb people had come to love the wide inter-vistas of open country and forest, and had continued to scatter their buildings, even after the necessity had passed. But the slim, towering buildings could only have been reared by a people who had banished nationalism and, with it, the threat of total war. He contrasted them with the ground-hugging dome cities of the Khiftan civilization, only a few thousand parayears distant.

Three men came out of the lounge behind him and joined him. One was, like himself, a disguised paratimer from the First Level—the Outtime Export and Import man, Zortan Brend, here known as Brarnend of Zorda. The other two were Akor-Neb people, and both wore the black tunics and the winged-bullet badges of the Society of Assassins. Unlike Verkan Vall and Zortan Brend, who wore shoulder holsters under their short tunics, the Assassins openly displayed pistols and knives on their belts.

"We heard that you were coming two days ago, Lord Virzal," Zortan Brend said. "We delayed the take-off of this ship, so that you could travel to Darsh as inconspicuously as possible. I also booked a suite for you at the Solar Hotel, at Darsh. And these are your Assassins—Olirzon, and Marnik."

Verkan Vall hooked fingers and clapped shoulders with them.

"Virzal of Verkan," he identified himself. "I am satisfied to intrust myself to you."

"We'll do our best for you, Lord Virzal," the older of the pair, Olirzon, said. He hesitated for a moment, then continued: "Understand, Lord Virzal, I only ask for information useful in serving and protecting you. But is this of the Lady Dallona a political matter?"

"Not from our side," Verkan Vall told him. "The Lady Dallona is a scientist, entirely nonpolitical. The Honorable Brarnend is a business man; he doesn't meddle with politics as long as the politicians leave him alone. And I'm a planter on Venus; I have enough troubles, with the natives, and the weather, and blue-rot in the *zerfa* plants, and poison roaches, and javelin bugs, without getting into politics. But psychic science is inextricably mixed with politics, and the Lady Dallona's work had evidently tended to discredit the theory of Statistical Reincarnation."

"Do you often make understatements like that, Lord Virzal?" Olirzon grinned. "In the last six months, she's knocked Statistical Reincarnation to splinters."

"Well, I'm not a psychic scientist, and as I said, I don't know much about Terran politics," Verkan Vall replied. "I know that the Statisticalists favor complete socialization and political control of the whole economy, because they want everybody to have the same opportunities in every reincarnation. And the Volitionalists believe that everybody reincarnates as he pleases, and so they favor continuance of the present system of private ownership of wealth and private profit under a system of free competition. And that's about all I do know. Naturally, as a landowner and the holder of a title of nobility, I'm a Volitionalist in politics, but the socialization issue isn't important on Venus. There is still too much unseated land there, and too many personal opportunities, to make socialism attractive to anybody."

"Well, that's about it," Zortan Brend told him. "I'm not enough of a psychicist to know what the Lady Dallona's been doing, but she's knocked the theoretical basis from under Statistical Reincarnation, and that's the basis, in turn, of Statistical Socialism. I think we'll find that the Statisticalist Party is responsible for whatever happened to her."

Marnik, the younger of the two Assassins, hesitated for a moment, then addressed Verkan Vall:

"Lord Virzal, I know none of the personalities involved in this matter, and I speak without wishing to give offense, but is it not possible that the Lady Dallona and the Assassin Dirzed may have gone somewhere together voluntarily? I have met Dirzed, and he has many qualities which women find attractive, and he is by no means indifferent to the opposite sex. You understand, Lord Virzal—"

"I understand all too perfectly, Marnik," Verkan Vall replied, out of the fullness of experience. "The Lady Dallona has had affairs with a number of men, myself among them. But under the circumstances, I find that explanation unthinkable."

Marnik looked at him in open skepticism. Evidently, in his book, where an attractive man and a beautiful woman were concerned, that explanation was never unthinkable.

"The Lady Dallona is a scientist," Verkan Vall elaborated. "She is not above diverting herself with love affairs, but that's all they are—a not too important form of diversion. And, if you recall, she had just participated in a most significant experiment: you can be sure that she had other things on her mind at the time than pleasure jaunts with good-looking Assassins."

The ship was passing around the Caucasus Mountains, with the Caspian Sea in sight ahead, when several of the crew appeared on the observation deck and began preparing the shielding to protect the deck from gunfire. Zortan Brend inquired of the petty officer in charge of the work as to the necessity.

"We've been getting reports of trouble at Darsh, sir," the man said. "Newscast bulletins every couple of minutes: rioting in different parts of the city. Started yesterday afternoon, when a couple of Statisticalist members of the Executive Council resigned and went over to the Volitionalists. Lord Nirzav of Shonna, the only nobleman of any importance in the Statisticalist Party, was one of them; he was shot immediately afterward, while leaving the Council Chambers, along with a couple of Assassins who were with him. Some people in an airboat sprayed them with a machine rifle as they came out onto the landing stage."

The two Assassins exclaimed in horrified anger over this.

"That wasn't the work of members of the Society of Assassins!" Olirzon declared. "Even after he'd resigned, the Lord Nirzav was still immune till he left the Government Building. There's too blasted much illegal assassination going on!"

"What happened next?" Verkan Vall wanted to know.

"About what you'd expect, sir. The Volitionalists weren't going to take that quietly. In the past eighteen hours, four prominent Statisticalists were forcibly discarnated, and there was even a fight in Mirzark of Bashad's house, when Volitionalist Assassins broke in; three of them and four of Mirzark's Assassins were discarnated."

"You know, something is going to have to be done about that, too," Olirzon said to Marnik. "It's getting to a point where these political faction fights are being carried on entirely between members of the Society. In Ghamma alone, last year, thirty or forty of our members were discarnated that way."

"Plug in a newscast visiplate, Karnil," Zortan Brend told the petty officer. "Let's see what's going on in Darsh now."

In Darsh, it seemed, an uneasy peace was being established. Verkan Vall watched heavily-armed airboats and light combat ships patrolling among the high towers of the city. He saw a couple of minor riots being broken up by the blue-uniformed Constabulary, with considerable shooting and a ruthless disregard for who might get shot. It wasn't exactly the sort of policing that would have been tolerated in the First Level Civil Order Section, but it seemed to suit Akor-Neb conditions. And he listened to a series of angry recriminations and contradictory statements by different politicians, all of whom blamed the disorders on their opponents. The Volitionalists spoke of the Statisticalists as "insane criminals" and "underminers of social stability," and the Statisticalists called the Volitionalists "reactionary criminals" and "enemies of social progress." Politicians, he had observed, differed little in their vocabularies from one time-line to another.

This kept up all the while the ship was passing over the Caspian Sea; as they were turning up the Volga valley, one of the ship's officers came down from the control deck, above.

"We're coming into Darsh, now," he said, and as Verkan Vall turned from the visiplate to the forward windows, he could see the white and pastel-tinted towers of the city rising above the hardwood forests that covered the whole Volga basin on this sector. "Your luggage has been put into the airboat, Lord Virzal and Honorable Assassins, and it's ready for launching whenever you are." The officer glanced at his watch. "We dock at Commercial Center in twenty minutes; we'll be passing the Solar Hotel in ten."

They all rose, and Verkan Vall hooked fingers and clapped shoulders with Zortan Brend.

"Good luck, Lord Virzal," the latter said. "I hope you find the Lady Dallona safe and carnate. If you need help, I'll be at Mercantile House for the next day or so; if you get back to Ghamma before I do, you know who to ask for there."

A number of assassins loitered in the hallways and offices of the Independent Institute of Reincarnation Research when Verkan Vall, accompanied by Marnik, called there that afternoon. Some of them carried submachine-guns or sleep-gas projectors, and they were stopping people and questioning them. Marnik needed only to give them a quick gesture and the words, "Assassins'

Truce," and he and his client were allowed to pass. They entered a lifter tube and floated up to the office of Dr. Harnosh of Hosh, with whom Verkan Vall had made an appointment.

"I'm sorry, Lord Virzal," the director of the Institute told him, "but I have no idea what has befallen the Lady Dallona, or even if she is still carnate. I am quite worried; I admired her extremely, both as an individual and as a scientist. I do hope she hasn't been discarnated; that would be a serious blow to science. It is fortunate that she accomplished as much as she did, while she was with us."

"You think she is no longer carnate, then?"

"I'm afraid so. The political effects of her discoveries—" Harnosh of Hosh shrugged sadly. "She was devoted, to a rare degree, to her work. I am sure that nothing but her discarnation could have taken her away from us, at this time, with so many important experiments still uncompleted."

Marnik nodded to Verkan Vall, as much as to say: "You were right."

"Well, I intend acting upon the assumption that she is still carnate and in need of help, until I am positive to the contrary," Verkan Vall said. "And in the latter case, I intend finding out who discarnated her, and send him to apologize for it in person. People don't forcibly discarnate my friends with impunity."

"Sound attitude," Dr. Harnosh commented. "There's certainly no positive evidence that she isn't still carnate. I'll gladly give you all the assistance I can, if you'll only tell me what you want."

"Well, in the first place," Verkan Vall began, "just what sort of work was she doing?" He already knew the answer to that, from the reports she had sent back to the First Level, but he wanted to hear Dr. Harnosh's version. "And what, exactly, are the political effects you mentioned? Understand, Dr. Harnosh, I am really quite ignorant of any scientific subject unrelated to *zerfa* culture, and equally so of Terran politics. Politics, on Venus, is mainly a question of who gets how much graft out of what."

Dr. Harnosh smiled; evidently he had heard about Venusian politics. "Ah, yes, of course. But you are familiar with the main differences between Statistical and Volitional reincarnation theories?"

"In a general way. The Volitionalists hold that the discarnate individuality is fully conscious, and is capable of something analogous to sense-perception, and is also capable of exercising choice in the matter of reincarnation vehicles, and can reincarnate or remain in the discarnate state as it chooses. They also believe that discarnate individualities can communicate with one another, and with at least some carnate individualities, by telepathy," he said. "The Statisticalists deny all this; their opinion is that the discarnate individuality is in a more or less somnambulistic state, that it is drawn by a process akin to tropism to the nearest available reincarnation vehicle, and that it must reincarnate in and only in that vehicle. They are labeled Statisticalists because they believe that the process of reincarnation is purely at random, or governed by unknown and uncontrollable causes, and is unpredictable except as to aggregates."

"That's a fairly good generalized summary," Dr. Harnosh of Hosh grudged, unwilling to give a mere layman too much credit. He dipped a spoon into a tobacco humidor, dusted the tobacco lightly with dried *zerfa*, and rammed it into his pipe. "You must understand that our modern Statisticalists are the intellectual heirs of those ancient materialistic thinkers who denied the possibility of any discarnate existence, or of any extraphysical mind, or even of extrasensory perception. Since all these things have been demonstrated to be facts, the materialistic dogma has been broadened to include them, but always strictly within the frame of materialism.

"We have proven, for instance, that the human individuality can exist in a discarnate state, and that it reincarnates into the body of an infant, shortly after birth. But the Statisticalists cannot accept the idea of discarnate consciousness, since they conceive of consciousness purely as a function of the physical brain. So they postulate an unconscious discarnate personality, or, as you put it, one in a somnambulistic state. They have to concede memory to this discarnate personality, since it was by recovery of memories of previous reincarnations that discarnate existence and reincarnation were proven to be facts. So they picture the discarnate individuality as a material object, or physical event, of negligible but actual mass, in which an indefinite number of memories can be stored as electronic charges. And they picture it as being drawn irresistibly to the body of the nearest non-incarnated infant. Curiously enough, the reincarnation vehicle chosen is almost always of the same sex as the vehicle of the previous reincarnation, the exceptions being cases of persons who had a previous history of psychological sex-inversion."

Dr. Harnosh remembered the unlighted pipe in his hand, thrust it into his mouth, and lit it. For a moment, he sat with it jutting out of his black beard, until it was drawing to his satisfaction. "This belief in immediate reincarnation leads the Statisticalists, when they fight duels or perform voluntary discarnation, to do so in the neighborhood of maternity hospitals," he added. "I know, personally, of one reincarnation memory-recall, in which the subject, a Statisticalist, voluntarily discarnated by lethal-gas inhaler in a private room at one of our local maternity hospitals, and reincarnated twenty years later in the city of Jeddul, three thousand miles away." The square black beard jiggled as the scientist laughed.

"Now, as to the political implications of these contradictory theories: Since the Statisticalists believe that they will reincarnate entirely at random, their aim is to create an utterly classless social and economic order, in which, theoretically, each individuality will reincarnate into a condition of equality with everybody else. Their political program, therefore, is one of complete socialization of all means of production and distribution, abolition of hereditary titles and inherited wealth—eventually, all private wealth—and total government control of all economic, social and cultural activities. Of course," Dr. Harnosh apologized, "politics isn't my subject; I wouldn't presume to judge how that would function in practice."

"I would," Verkan Vall said shortly, thinking of all the different time-lines on which he had seen systems like that in operation. "You wouldn't like it, doctor. And the Volitionalists?"

"Well, since they believe that they are able to choose the circumstances of their next reincarnations for themselves, they are the party of the *status quo*. Naturally, almost all the nobles, almost all the wealthy trading and manufacturing families, and almost all professional people, are Volitionalists; most of the workers and peasants are Statisticalists. Or, at least, they were, for the most part, before we began announcing the results of the Lady Dallona's experimental work."

"Ah; now we come to it," Verkan Vall said as the story clarified.

"Yes. In somewhat oversimplified form, the situation is rather like this," Dr. Harnosh of Hosh said. "The Lady Dallona introduced a number of refinements and some outright innovations into our technique of recovering memories of past reincarnations. Previously, it was necessary to keep the subject in an hypnotic trance, during which he or she would narrate what was remembered of past reincarnations, and this would be recorded. On emerging from the trance, the subject would remember nothing; the tape-recording would be all that would be left. But the Lady Dallona devised a technique by which these memories would remain in what might be called the fore part of the subject's subconscious mind, so that they could be brought to the level of consciousness at will. More, she was able to recover memories of past discarnate existences, something we had never been able to do heretofore." Dr. Harnosh shook his head. "And to think, when I first met her, I thought that she was just another sensation-seeking young lady of wealth, and was almost about to refuse her enrollment!"

He wasn't the only one whom little Dalla had surprised, Verkan Vall thought. At least, he had been pleasantly surprised.

"You see, this entirely disproves the Statistical Theory of Reincarnation. For example, we got a fine set of memory-recalls from one subject, for four previous reincarnations and four intercarnations. In the first of these, the subject had been a peasant on the estate of a wealthy noble. Unlike most of his fellows, who reincarnated into other peasant families almost immediately after discarnation, this man waited for fifty years in the discarnate state for an opportunity to reincarnate as the son of an over-servant. In his next reincarnation, he was the son of a technician, and received a technical education; he became a physics researcher. For his next reincarnation, he chose the son of a nobleman by a concubine as his vehicle; in his present reincarnation, he is a member of a wealthy manufacturing family, and married into a family of the nobility. In five reincarnations, he has climbed from the lowest to the next-to-highest rung of the social ladder. Few individuals of the class from whence he began this ascent possess so much persistence or determination. Then, of course, there was the case of Lord Garnon of Roxor."

He went on to describe the last experiment in which Hadron Dalla had participated.

"Well, that all sounds pretty conclusive," Verkan Vall commented. "I take it the leaders of the Volitionalist Party here are pleased with the result of the Lady Dallona's work?"

"Pleased? My dear Lord Virzal, they're fairly bursting with glee over it!" Harnosh of Hosh declared. "As I pointed out, the Statisticalist program of socialization is based entirely on the proposition that no one can choose the circumstances of his next reincarnation, and that's been demonstrated to be utter nonsense. Until the Lady Dallona's discoveries were announced, they were the dominant party, controlling a majority of the seats in Parliament and on the Executive Council. Only the Constitution kept them from enacting their entire socialization program long ago, and they were about to legislate constitutional changes which would remove that barrier. They had expected to be able to do so after the forthcoming general elections. But now, social inequality has become desirable: it gives people something to look forward to in the next reincarnation. Instead of wanting to abolish wealth and privilege and nobility, the proletariat want to reincarnate into them." Harnosh of Hosh laughed happily. "So you can see how furious the Statisticalist Party organization is!"

"There's a catch to this, somewhere," Marnik the Assassin, speaking for the first time, declared. "They can't all reincarnate as princes, there aren't enough vacancies to go 'round. And no noble is going to reincarnate as a tractor driver to make room for a tractor driver who wants to reincarnate as a noble."

"That's correct," Dr. Harnosh replied. "There is a catch to it; a catch most people would never admit, even to themselves. Very few individuals possess the will power, the intelligence or the capacity for mental effort displayed by the subject of the case I just quoted. The average man's interests are almost entirely on the physical side; he actually finds mental effort painful, and makes as little of it as possible. And that is the only sort of effort a discarnate individuality can exert. So, unable to endure the fifty or so years needed to make a really good reincarnation, he reincarnates in a year or so, out of pure boredom, into the first vehicle he can find, usually one nobody else wants." Dr. Harnosh dug out the heel of his pipe and blew through the stem. "But nobody will admit his own mental inferiority, even to himself. Now, every machine operator and field hand on the planet thinks he can reincarnate as a prince or a millionaire. Politics isn't my subject, but I'm willing to bet that since Statistical Reincarnation is an exploded psychic theory, Statisticalist Socialism has been caught in the blast area and destroyed along with it.

Olirzon was in the drawing room of the hotel suite when they returned, sitting on the middle of his spinal column in a reclining chair, smoking a pipe, dressing the edge of his knife with a pocket-hone, and gazing lecherously at a young woman in the visiplate. She was an extremely well-designed young woman, in a rather fragmentary costume, and she was heaving her bosom at the invisible audience in anger, sorrow, scorn, entreaty, and numerous other emotions.

"... this revolting crime," she was declaiming, in a husky contralto, as Verkan Vall and Marnik entered, "foul even for the criminal beasts who conceived and perpetrated it!" She pointed an accusing finger. "This murder of the beautiful Lady Dallona of Hadron!"

Verkan Vall stopped short, considering the possibility of something having been discovered lately of which he was ignorant. Olirzon must have guessed his thought; he grinned reassuringly.

"Think nothing of it, Lord Virzal," he said, waving his knife at the visiplate. "Just political propaganda; strictly for the sparrows. Nice propagandist, though."

"And now," the woman with the magnificent natural resources lowered her voice reverently, "we bring you the last image of the Lady Dallona, and of Dirzed, her faithful Assassin, taken just before they vanished, never to be seen again."

The plate darkened, and there were strains of slow, dirgelike music; then it lighted again, presenting a view of a broad hallway, thronged with men and women in bright varicolored costumes. In the foreground, wearing a tight skirt of deep blue and a short red jacket, was Hadron Dalla, just as she had looked in the solidographs taken in Dhergabar after her alteration by the First Level cosmeticians to conform to the appearance of the Malayoid Akor-Neb people. She was holding the arm of a man who wore the black tunic and red badge of an Assassin, a handsome specimen of the Akor-Neb race. Trust little Dalla for that, Verkan Vall thought. The figures were moving with exaggerated slowness, as though a very fleeting picture were being stretched out as far as possible. Having already memorized his former wife's changed appearance, Verkan Vall concentrated on the man beside her until the picture faded.

"All right, Olirzon; what did you get?" he asked.

"Well, first of all, at Assassins' Hall," Olirzon said, rolling up his left sleeve, holding his bare forearm to the light, and shaving a few fine hairs from it to test the edge of his knife. "Of course, they never tell one Assassin anything about the client of another Assassin; that's standard practice. But I was in the Lodge Secretary's office, where nobody but Assassins are ever admitted. They have a big panel in there, with the names of all the Lodge members on it in light-letters; that's standard in all Lodges. If an Assassin is unattached and free to accept a client, his name's in white light. If he has a client, the light's changed to blue, and the name of the client goes up under his. If his whereabouts are unknown, the light's changed to amber. If he is discarnated, his name's removed entirely, unless the circumstances of his discarnation are such as to constitute an injury to the Society. In that case, the name's in red light until he's been properly avenged, or, as we say, till his blood's been mopped up. Well, the name of Dirzed is up in blue light, with the name of

Dallona of Hadron under it. I found out that the light had been amber for two days after the disappearance, and then had been changed back to blue. Get it, Lord Virzal?"

Verkan Vall nodded. "I think so. I'd been considering that as a possibility from the first. Then what?"

"Then I was about and around for a couple of hours, buying drinks for people—unattached Assassins, Constabulary detectives, political workers, newscast people. You owe me fifteen System Monetary Units for that, Lord Virzal. What I got, when it's all sorted out—I taped it in detail, as soon as I got back—reduces to this: The Volitionalists are moving mountains to find out who was the spy at Garnon of Roxor's discarnation feast, but are doing nothing but nothing at all to find the Lady Dallona or Dirzed. The Statisticalists are making all sorts of secret efforts to find out what happened to her. The Constabulary blame the Statistos for the package-bomb: they're interested in that because of the discarnation of the three servants by an illegal weapon of indiscriminate effect. They claim that the disappearance of Dirzed and the Lady Dallona was a publicity hoax. The Volitionalists are preparing a line of publicity to deny this."

Verkan Vall nodded. "That ties in with what you learned at Assassins' Hall," he said. "They're hiding out somewhere. Is there any chance of reaching Dirzed through the Society of Assassins?"

Olirzon shook his head. "If you're right—and that's the way it looks to me, too—he's probably just called in and notified the Society that he's still carnate and so is the Lady Dallona, and called off any search the Society might be making for him."

"And I've got to find the Lady Dallona as soon as I can. Well, if I can't reach her, maybe I can get her to send word to me," Verkan Vall said. "That's going to take some doing, too."

"What did you find out, Lord Virzal?" Olirzon asked. He had a piece of soft leather, now, and was polishing his blade lovingly.

"The Reincarnation Research people don't know anything," Verkan Vall replied. "Dr. Harnosh of Hosh thinks she's discarnate. I did find out that the experimental work she's done, so far, has absolutely disproved the theory of Statistical Reincarnation. The Volitionalists' theory is solidly established."

"Yes, what do you think, Olirzon?" Marnik added. "They have a case on record of a man who worked up from field hand to millionaire in five reincarnations. Deliberately, that is." He went on to repeat what Harnosh of Hosh had said; he must have possessed an almost eidetic memory, for he gave the bearded psychicist's words verbatim, and threw in the gestures and voice-inflections.

Olirzon grinned. "You know, there's a chance for the easy-money boys," he considered. "'You, too, can Reincarnate as a millionaire! Let Dr. Nirzutz of Futzbutz Help You! Only 49.98 System Monetary Units for the Secret, Infallible, Autosuggestive Formula.' And would it sell!" He put away the hone and the bit of leather and slipped his knife back into its sheath. "If I weren't a respectable Assassin, I'd give it a try, myself."

Verkan Vall looked at his watch. "We'd better get something to eat," he said. "We'll go down to the main dining room; the Martian Room, I think they call it. I've got to think of some way to let the Lady Dallona know I'm looking for her."

The Martian Room, fifteen stories down, was a big place, occupying almost half of the floor space of one corner tower. It had been fitted to resemble one of the ruined buildings of the ancient and vanished race of Mars who were the ancestors of Terran humanity. One whole side of the room was a gigantic cine-solidograph screen, on which the gullied desolation of a Martian landscape was projected; in the course of about two hours, the scene changed from sunrise through daylight and night to sunrise again.

It was high noon when they entered and found a table; by the time they had finished their dinner, the night was ending and the first glow of dawn was tinting the distant hills. They sat for a while, watching the light grow stronger, then got up and left the table.

There were five men at a table near them; they had come in before the stars had grown dim, and the waiters were just bringing their first dishes. Two were Assassins, and the other three were of a breed Verkan Vall had learned to recognize on any time-line—the arrogant, cocksure, ambitious, leftist politician, who knows what is best for everybody better than anybody else does, and who is convinced that he is inescapably right and that whoever differs with him is not only an ignoramus but a venal scoundrel as well. One was a beefy man in a gold-laced cream-colored dress tunic; he had thick lips and a too-ready laugh. Another was a rather monkish-looking young man who spoke earnestly and rolled his eyes upward, as though at some celestial vision. The third had the faint powdering of gray in his black hair which was, among the Akor-Neb people, almost the only indication of advanced age.

"Of course it is; the whole thing is a fraud," the monkish young man was saying angrily. "But we can't prove it."

"Oh, Sirzob, here, can prove anything, if you give him time," the beefy one laughed. "The trouble is, there isn't too much time. We know that that communication was a fake, prearranged by the Volitionalists, with Dr. Harnosh and this Dallona of Hadron as their tools. They fed the whole thing to that idiot boy hypnotically, in advance, and then, on a signal, he began typing out this spurious communication. And then, of course, Dallona and this Assassin of hers ran off somewhere together, so that we'd be blamed with discarnating or abducting them, and so that they wouldn't be made to testify about the communication on a lie detector."

A sudden happy smile touched Verkan Vall's eyes. He caught each of his Assassins by an arm.

"Marnik, cover my back," he ordered. "Olirzon, cover everybody at the table. Come on!"

Then he stepped forward, halting between the chairs of the young man and the man with the gray hair and facing the beefy man in the light tunic.

"You!" he barked. "I mean YOU."

The beefy man stopped laughing and stared at him; then sprang to his feet. His hand, streaking toward his left armpit, stopped and dropped to his side as Olirzon aimed a pistol at him. The others sat motionless.

"You," Verkan Vall continued, "are a complete, deliberate, malicious, and unmitigated liar. The Lady Dallona of Hadron is a scientist of integrity, incapable of falsifying her experimental work. What's more, her father is one of my best friends; in his name, and in hers, I demand a full retraction of the slanderous statements you have just made."

"Do you know who I am?" the beefy one shouted.

"I know *what* you are," Verkan Vall shouted back. Like most ancient languages, the Akor-Neb speech included an elaborate, delicately-shaded, and utterly vile vocabulary of abuse; Verkan Vall culled from it judiciously and at length. "And if I don't make myself understood verbally, we'll go down to the object level," he added, snatching a bowl of soup from in front of the monkish-looking young man and throwing it across the table.

The soup was a dark brown, almost black. It contained bits of meat, and mushrooms, and slices of hard-boiled egg, and yellow Martian rock lichen. It produced, on the light tunic, a most spectacular effect.

For a moment, Verkan Vall was afraid the fellow would have an apoplectic stroke, or an epileptic fit. Mastering himself, however, he bowed jerkily.

"Marnark of Bashad," he identified himself. "When

and where can my friends consult yours?"

"Lord Virzal of Verkan," the paratimer bowed back. "Your friends can negotiate with mine here and now. I am represented by these Gentlemen-Assassins."

"I won't submit my friends to the indignity of negotiating with them," Marnark retorted. "I insist that you be represented by persons of your own quality and mine."

"Oh, you do?" Olirzon broke in. "Well, is your objection personal to me, or to Assassins as a class? In the first case, I'll remember to make a private project of you, as soon as I'm through with my present employment; if it's the latter, I'll report your attitude to the Society. I'll see what Klarnood, our President-General, thinks of your views."

A crowd had begun to accumulate around the table. Some of them were persons in evening dress, some were Assassins on the hotel payroll, and some were unattached Assassins.

"Well, you won't have far to look for him," one of the latter said, pushing through the crowd to the table.

He was a man of middle age, inclined to stoutness; he made Verkan Vall think of a chocolate figure of Tortha Karf. The red badge on his breast was surrounded with gold lace, and, instead of black wings and a silver bullet, it bore silver wings and a golden dagger. He bowed contemptuously at Marnark of Bashad.

"Klarnood, President-General of the Society of Assassins," he announced. "Marnark of Bashad, did I hear you say that you considered members of the Society as unworthy to negotiate an affair of honor with your friends, on behalf of this nobleman who has been courteous enough to accept your challenge?" he demanded.

Marnark of Bashad's arrogance suffered considerable evaporation-loss. His tone became almost servile.

"Not at all, Honorable Assassin-President," he protested. "But as I was going to ask these gentlemen to represent me, I thought it would be more fitting for the other gentleman to be represented by personal friends, also. In that way—"

"Sorry, Marnark," the gray-haired man at the table said. "I can't second you; I have a quarrel with the Lord Virzal, too." He rose and bowed. "Sirzob of Abo. Inasmuch as the Honorable Marnark is a guest at my table, an affront to him is an affront to me. In my quality as his host, I must demand satisfaction from you, Lord Virzal."

"Why, gladly, Honorable Sirzob," Verkan Vall replied. This was getting better and better every moment. "Of course, your friend, the Honorable Marnark, enjoys priority of challenge; I'll take care of you as soon as I have, shall we say, satisfied, him."

The earnest and rather consecrated-looking young man rose also, bowing to Verkan Vall.

"Yirzol of Narva. I, too, have a quarrel with you, Lord Virzal; I cannot submit to the indignity of having my food snatched from in front of me, as you just did. I also demand satisfaction."

"And quite rightly, Honorable Yirzol," Verkan Vall approved. "It looks like such good soup, too," he sorrowed, inspecting the front of Marnark's tunic. "My seconds will negotiate with yours immediately; your satisfaction, of course, must come after that of Honorable Sirzob."

"If I may intrude," Klarnood put in smoothly, "may I suggest that as the Lord Virzal is represented by his Assassins, yours can represent all three of you at the same time. I will gladly offer my own good offices as impartial supervisor."

Verkan Vall turned and bowed as to royalty. "An honor, Assassin-President: I am sure no one could act in that capacity more satisfactorily."

"Well, when would it be most convenient to arrange the details?" Klarnood inquired. "I am completely at your disposal, gentlemen."

"Why, here and now, while we're all together," Verkan Vall replied.

"I object to that!" Marnark of Bashad vociferated. "We can't make arrangements here; why, all these hotel people, from the manager down, are nothing but tipsters for the newscast services!"

"Well, what's wrong with that?" Verkan Vall demanded. "You knew that when you slandered the Lady Dallona in their hearing."

"The Lord Virzal of Verkan is correct," Klarnood ruled. "And the offenses for which you have challenged him were also committed in public. By all means, let's discuss the arrangements now." He turned to Verkan Vall. "As the challenged party, you have the choice of weapons; your opponents, then, have the right to name the conditions under which they are to be used."

Marnark of Bashad raised another outcry over that. The assault upon him by the Lord Virzal of Verkan was deliberately provocative, and therefore tantamount to a challenge; he, himself, had the right to name the weapons. Klarnood upheld him.

"Do the other gentlemen make the same claim?" Verkan Vall wanted to know.

"If they do, I won't allow it," Klarnood replied. "You deliberately provoked Honorable Marnark, but the offenses of provoking him at Honorable Sirzob's table, and of throwing Honorable Yirzol's soup at him, were not given with intent to provoke. These gentlemen have a right to challenge, but not to consider themselves provoked."

"Well, I choose knives, then," Marnark hastened to say.

Verkan Vall smiled thinly. He had learned knife-play among the greatest masters of that art in all paratime, the Third Level Khanga pirates of the Caribbean Islands.

"And we fight barefoot, stripped to the waist, and without any parrying weapon in the left hand," Verkan Vall stipulated.

The beefy Marnark fairly licked his chops in anticipation. He outweighed Verkan Vall by forty pounds; he saw an easy victory ahead. Verkan Vall's own confidence increased at these signs of his opponent's assurance.

"And as for Honorable Sirzob and Honorable Yirzol, I chose pistols," he added.

Sirzob and Yirzol held a hasty whispered conference.

"Speaking both for Honorable Yirzol and for myself," Sirzob announced, "we stipulate that the distance shall be twenty meters, that the pistols shall be fully loaded, and that fire shall be at will after the command."

"Twenty rounds, fire at will, at twenty meters!" Olirzon hooted. "You must think our principal's as bad a shot as you are!"

The four Assassins stepped aside and held a long discussion about something, with considerable argument and gesticulation. Klarnood, observing Verkan Vall's impatience, leaned close to him and whispered:

"This is highly irregular; we must pretend ignorance and be patient. They're laying bets on the outcome. You must do your best, Lord Virzal; you don't want your supporters to lose money."

He said it quite seriously, as though the outcome were otherwise a matter of indifference to Verkan Vall.

Marnark wanted to discuss time and place, and proposed that all three duels be fought at dawn, on the fourth landing stage of Darsh Central Hospital; that was closest to the maternity wards, and statistics showed that most births occurred just before that hour.

"Certainly not," Verkan Vall vetoed. "We'll fight here and now; I don't propose going a couple of hundred miles to meet you at any such unholy hour. We'll fight in the nearest hallway that provides twenty meters' shooting distance."

Marnark, Sirzob and Yirzol all clamored in protest. Verkan Vall shouted them down, drawing on his hypnotically acquired knowledge of Akor-Neb duelling customs.

"The code explicitly states that satisfaction shall be rendered as promptly as possible, and I insist on a literal interpretation. I'm not going to inconvenience myself and Assassin-President Klarnood and these four Gentlemen-Assassins just to humor Statisticalist superstitions."

The manager of the hotel, drawn to the Martian Room by the uproar, offered a hallway connecting the kitchens with the refrigerator rooms; it was fifty meters long by five in width, was well-lighted and soundproof, and had a bay in which the seconds and other could stand during the firing.

They repaired thither in a body, Klarnood gathering up several hotel servants on the way through the kitchen. Verkan Vall stripped to the waist, pulled off his ankle boots, and examined Olirzon's knife. Its tapering eight-inch blade was double-edged at the point, and its handle was covered with black velvet to afford a good grip, and wound with gold wire. He nodded approvingly, gripped it with his index finger crooked around the cross-guard, and advanced to meet Marnark of Bashad.

As he had expected, the burly politician was depending upon his greater brawn to overpower his antagonist. He advanced with a sidling, spread-legged gait, his knife hand against his right hip and his left hand extended in front. Verkan Vall nodded with pleased satisfaction; a wrist-grabber. Then he blinked. Why, the fellow was actually holding his knife reversed, his little finger to the guard and his thumb on the pommel!

Verkan Vall went briskly to meet him, made a feint at his knife hand with his own left, and then side-stepped quickly to the right. As Marnark's left hand grabbed at his right wrist, his left hand brushed against it and closed into a fist, with Marnark's left thumb inside of it, He gave a quick downward twist with his wrist, pulling Marnark off balance.

Caught by surprise, Marnark stumbled, his knife flailing wildly away from Verkan Vall. As he stumbled forward, Verkan Vall pivoted on his left heel and drove the point of his knife into the back of Marnark's neck, twisting it as he jerked it free. At the same time, he released Marnark's thumb. The politician continued his stumble and fell forward on his face, blood spurting from his neck. He gave a twitch or so, and was still.

Verkan Vall stooped and wiped the knife on the dead man's clothes—another Khanga pirate gesture—and then returned it to Olirzon.

"Nice weapon, Olirzon," he said. "It fitted my hand as though I'd been born holding it."

"You used it as though you had, Lord Virzal," the Assassin replied. "Only eight seconds from the time you closed with him."

The function of the hotel servants whom Klarnood had gathered up now became apparent; they advanced, took the body of Marnark by the heels, and dragged it out of the way. The others watched this removal with mixed emotions. The two remaining principals were impassive and frozen-faced. Their two Assassins, who had probably bet heavily on Marnark, were chagrined. And Klarnood was looking at Verkan Vall with a considerable accretion of respect. Verkan Vall pulled on his boots and resumed his clothing.

There followed some argument about the pistols; it was finally decided that each combatant should use his own shoulder-holster weapon. All three were nearly enough alike—small weapons, rather heavier than they looked, firing a tiny ten-grain bullet at ten thousand foot-seconds. On impact, such a bullet would almost disintegrate; a man hit anywhere in the body with one would be killed instantly, his nervous system paralyzed and his heart stopped by internal pressure. Each of the pistols carried twenty rounds in the magazine.

Verkan Vall and Sirzob of Abo took their places, their pistols lowered at their sides, facing each other across a measured twenty meters.

"Are you ready, gentlemen?" Klarnood asked. "You will not raise your pistols until the command to fire; you may fire at will after it. Ready. *Fire!*"

Both pistols swung up to level. Verkan Vall found Sirzob's head in his sights and squeezed; the pistol kicked back in his hand, and he saw a lance of blue flame jump from the muzzle of Sirzob's. Both weapons barked together, and with the double report came the whip-cracking sound of Sirzob's bullet passing Verkan Vall's head. Then Sirzob's face altered its appearance unpleasantly, and he pitched forward. Verkan Vall thumbed on his safety and stood motionless, while the servants advanced, took Sirzob's body by the heels, and dragged it over beside Marnark's.

"All right; Honorable Yirzol, you're next," Verkan Vall called out.

"The Lord Virzal has fired one shot," one of the opposing seconds objected, "and Honorable Yirzol has a full magazine. The Lord Virzal should put in another magazine."

"I grant him the advantage; let's get on with it," Verkan Vall said.

Yirzol of Narva advanced to the firing point. He was not afraid of death—none of the Akor-Neb people were; their language contained no word to express the concept of total and final extinction—and discarnation by gunshot was almost entirely painless. But he was beginning to suspect that he had made a fool of himself by getting into this affair, he had work in his present reincarnation which he wanted to finish, and his political party would suffer loss, both of his services and of prestige.

"Are you ready, gentlemen?" Klarnood intoned ritualistically. "You will not raise your pistols until the command to fire; you may fire at will after it. Ready, *Fire!*"

Verkan Vall shot Yirzol of Narva through the head before the latter had his pistol half raised. Yirzol fell forward on the splash of blood Sirzob had made, and the servants came forward and dragged his body over with the others. It reminded Verkan Vail of some sort of industrial assembly-line operation. He replaced the two expended rounds in his magazine with fresh ones and slid the pistol back into its holster. The two Assassins whose principals had been so expeditiously massacred were beginning to count up their losses and pay off the winners.

Klarnood, the President-General of the Society of Assassins, came over, hooking fingers and clapping shoulders with Verkan Vall.

"Lord Virzal, I've seen quite a few duels, but nothing quite like that," he said. "You should have been an Assassin!"

That was a considerable compliment. Verkan Vall thanked him modestly.

"I'd like to talk to you privately," the Assassin-President continued. "I think it'll be worth your while if we have a few words together."

Verkan Vall nodded. "My suite is on the fifteenth floor above; will that be all right?" He waited until the losers had finished settling their bets, then motioned to his own pair of Assassins.

As they emerged into the Martian Room again, the manager was waiting; he looked as though he were about to demand that Verkan Vall vacate his suite. However, when he saw the arm of the President-General of the Society of Assassins draped amicably over his guest's shoulder, he came forward bowing and smiling.

"Larnorm, I want you to put five of your best Assassins to guarding the approaches to the Lord Virzal's suite," Klarnood told him. "I'll send five more from Assassins' Hall to replace them at their ordinary duties. And I'll hold you responsible with your carnate existence for the Lord Virzal's safety in this hotel. Understand?"

"Oh, yes, Honorable Assassin-President; you may trust me. The Lord Virzal will be perfectly safe."

In Verkan Vall's suite, above, Klarnood sat down and

got out his pipe, filling it with tobacco lightly mixed with *zerfa*. To his surprise, he saw his host light a plain tobacco cigarette.

"Don't you use *zerfa*?" he asked.

"Very little," Verkan Vall replied. "I grow it. If you'd see the bums who hang around our drying sheds, on Venus, cadging rejected leaves and smoking themselves into a stupor, you'd be frugal in using it, too."

Klarnood nodded. "You know, most men would want a pipe of fifty percent, or a straight *zerfa* cigarette, after what you've been through," he said.

"I'd need something like that, to deaden my conscience, if I had one to deaden," Verkan Vall said. "As it is, I feel like a murderer of babes. That overgrown fool, Marnark, handled his knife like a cow-butcher. The young fellow couldn't handle a pistol at all. I suppose the old fellow, Sirzob, was a fair shot, but dropping him wasn't any great feat of arms, either."

Klarnood looked at him curiously for a moment. "You know," he said, at length, "I believe you actually mean that. Well, until he met you, Marnark of Bashad was rated as the best knife-fighter in Darsh. Sirzob had ten dueling victories to his credit, and young Yirzol four." He puffed slowly on his pipe. "I like you, Lord Virzal; a great Assassin was lost when you decided to reincarnate as a Venusian land-owner. I'd hate to see you discarnated without proper warning. I take it you're ignorant of the intricacies of Terran politics?"

"To a large extent, yes."

"Well, do you know who those three men were?" When Verkan Vall shook his head, Klarnood continued: "Marnark was the son and right-hand associate of old Mirzark of Bashad, the Statisticalist Party leader. Sirzob of Abo was their propaganda director. And Yirzol of Narva was their leading socio-economic theorist, and their candidate for Executive Chairman. In six minutes, with one knife thrust and two shots, you did the Statisticalist Party an injury second only to that done them by the young lady in whose name you were fighting. In two weeks, there will be a planet-wide general election. As it stands, the Statisticalists have a majority of the seats in Parliament and on the Executive Council. As a result of your work and the Lady Dallona's, they'll lose that majority, and more, when the votes are tallied."

"Is that another reason why you like me?" Verkan Vall asked.

"Unofficially, yes. As President-General of the Society of Assassins, I must be nonpolitical. The Society is rigidly so; if we let ourselves become involved, as an organization, in politics, we could control the System Government inside of five years, and we'd be wiped out of existence in fifty years by the very forces we sought to control," Klarnood said. "But personally, I would like to see the Statisticalist Party destroyed. If they succeed in their program of socialization, the Society would be finished. A socialist state is, in its final development, an absolute, total, state; no total state can tolerate extra-legal and para-governmental organizations. So we have adopted the policy of giving a little inconspicuous aid, here and there, to people who are dangerous to the Statisticalists. The Lady Dallona of Hadron, and Dr. Harnosh of Hosh, are such persons. You appear to be another. That's why I ordered that fellow, Larnorm, to make sure you were safe in his hotel."

"Where is the Lady Dallona?" Verkan Vall asked. "From your use of the present tense, I assume you believe her to be still carnate."

Klarnood looked at Verkan Vall keenly. "That's a pretty blunt question, Lord Virzal," he said. "I wish I knew a little more about you. When you and your Assassins started inquiring about the Lady Dallona, I tried to check up on you. I found out that you had come to Darsh from Ghamma on a ship of the family of Zorda, accompanied by Brarnend of Zorda himself. And that's all I could find out. You claim to be a Venusian planter, and you might be. Any Terran who can handle weapons as you can would have come to my notice long ago. But you have no more ascertainable history than if you'd stepped out of another dimension."

That was getting uncomfortably close to the truth. In fact, it *was* the truth. Verkan Vall laughed.

"Well, confidentially," he said, "I'm from the Arcturus System. I followed the Lady Dallona here from our home planet, and when I have rescued her from among you Solarians, I shall, according to our customs, receive her hand in marriage. As she is the daughter of the Emperor of Arcturus, that'll be quite a good thing for me."

Klarnood chuckled. "You know, you'd only have to tell me that about three or four times and I'd start believing it," he said. "And Dr. Harnosh of Hosh would believe it the first time; he's been talking to himself ever since the Lady Dallona started her experimental work here. Lord Virzal, I'm going to take a chance on you. The Lady Dallona is still carnate, or was four days ago, and the same for Dirzed. They both went into hiding after the discarnation feast of Garnon of Roxor, to escape the enmity of the Statisticalists. Two days after they disappeared, Dirzed called Assassins' Hall and reported this, but told us nothing more. I suppose, in about three or four days, I could re-establish contact with him. We want the public to think that the Statisticalists made away with the Lady Dallona, at least until the election's over."

Verkan Vall nodded. "I was pretty sure that was the situation," he said. "It may be that they will get in touch with me; if they don't, I'll need your help in reaching them."

"Why do you think the Lady Dallona will try to reach you?"

"She needs all the help she can get. She knows she can get plenty from me. Why do you think I interrupted my search for her, and risked my carnate existence, to fight those people over a matter of verbalisms and political propaganda?" Verkan Vall went to the newscast visiplate and snapped it on. "We'll see if I'm getting results, yet."

The plate lighted, and a handsome young man in a gold-laced green suit was speaking out of it:

"... where he is heavily guarded by Assassins. However, in an exclusive interview with representatives of this service, the Assassin Hirzif, one of the two who seconded the men the Lord Virzal fought, said that in his opinion all of the three were so outclassed as to have had no chance whatever, and that he had already refused an offer of ten thousand System Monetary Units to discarnate the Lord Virzal for the Statisticalist Party. 'When I want to discarnate,' Hirzif the Assassin said, 'I'll invite in my friends and do it properly; until I do, I wouldn't go up against the Lord Virzal of Verkan for ten million S.M.U.'"

Verkan Vall snapped off the visiplate. "See what I mean?" he asked. "I fought those politicians just for the advertising. If Dallona and Dirzed are anywhere near a visiplate, they'll know how to reach me."

"Hirzif shouldn't have talked about refusing that retainer," Klarnood frowned. "That isn't good Assassin ethics. Why, yes, Lord Virzal; that was cleverly planned. It ought to get results. But I wish you'd get the Lady Dallona out of Darsh, and preferably off Terra, as soon as you can. We've benefited by this, so far, but I shouldn't like to see things go much further. A real civil war could develop out of this situation, and I don't want that. Call on me for help; I'll give you a code word to use at Assassins' Hall."

A real civil war was developing even as Klarnood spoke; by mid-morning of the next day, the fighting that had been partially suppressed by the Constabulary had broken out anew. The Assassins employed by the Solar Hotel—heavily re-enforced during the night—had fought a pitched battle with Statisticalist partisans on the landing-stage above Verkan Vall's suite, and now several

Constabulary airboats were patrolling around the building. The rule on Constabulary interference seemed to be that while individuals had an unquestionable right to shoot out their differences among themselves, any fighting likely to endanger nonparticipants was taboo.

Just how successful in enforcing this rule the Constabulary were was open to some doubt. Ever since arising, Verkan Vall had heard the crash of small arms and the hammering of automatic weapons in other parts of the towering city-unit. There hadn't been a civil war on the Akor-Neb Sector for over five centuries, he knew, but then, Hadron Dalla, Doctor of Psychic Science, and intertemporal trouble-carrier extraordinary, had only been on this sector for a little under a year. If anything, he was surprised that the explosion had taken so long to occur.

One of the servants furnished to him by the hotel management approached him in the drawing room, holding a four-inch-square wafer of white plastic.

"Lord Virzal, there is a masked Assassin in the hallway who brought this under Assassins' Truce," he said.

Verkan Vall took the wafer and pared off three of the four edges, which showed black where they had been fused. Unfolding it, he found, as he had expected, that the pyrographed message within was in the alphabet and language of the First Paratime Level:

> Vall, darling:
>   Am I glad you got here; this time I really *am* in the middle, but good! The Assassin, Dirzed, who brings this, is in my service. You can trust him implicitly; he's about the only person in Dash you can trust. He'll bring you to where I am.
>   Dalla
>
> P.S. I hope you're not still angry about that musician. I told you, at the time, that he was just helping me with an experiment in telepathy.
>   D.

Verkan Vall grinned at the postscript. That had been twenty years ago, when he'd been eighty and she'd been seventy. He supposed she'd expect him to take up his old relationship with her again. It probably wouldn't last any longer than it had, the other time; he recalled a Fourth Level proverb about the leopard and his spots. It certainly wouldn't be boring, though.

"Tell the Assassin to come in," he directed. Then he tossed the message down on a table. Outside of himself, nobody in Darsh could read it but the woman who had sent it; if, as he thought highly probable, the Statisticalists had spies among the hotel staff, it might serve to reduce some cryptanalyst to gibbering insanity.

The Assassin entered, drawing off a cowllike mask. He was the man whose arm Dalla had been holding in the visiplate picture; Verkan Vall even recognized the extremely ornate pistol and knife on his belt.

"Dirzed the Assassin," he named himself. "If you wish, we can visiphone Assassins' Hall for verification of my identity."

"Lord Virzal of Verkan. And my Assassins, Marnik and Olirzon." They all hooked fingers and clapped shoulders with the newcomer. "That won't be needed," Verkan Vall told Dirzed. "I know you from seeing you with the Lady Dallona, on the visiplate; you're 'Dirzed, her faithful Assassin.'"

Dirzed's face, normally the color of a good walnut gunstock, turned almost black. He used shockingly bad language.

"And that's why I have to wear this abomination," he finished, displaying the mask. "The Lady Dallona and I can't show our faces anywhere; if we did, every Statisticalist and his six-year-old brat would know us, and we'd be fighting off an army of them in five minutes."

"Where's the Lady Dallona, now?"

"In hiding, Lord Virzal, at a private dwelling dome in the forest; she's most anxious to see you. I'm to take you to her, and I would strongly advise that you bring your Assassins along. There are other people at this dome, and they are not personally loyal to the Lady Dallona. I've no reason to suspect them of secret enmity, but their friendship is based entirely on political expediency."

"And political expediency is subject to change without notice," Verkan Vall finished for him. "Have you an airboat?"

"On the landing stage below. Shall we go now, Lord Virzal?"

"Yes." Verkan Vall made a two-handed gesture to his Assassins, as though gripping a submachine-gun; they nodded, went into another room, and returned carrying light automatic weapons in their hands and pouches of spare drums slung over their shoulders. "And may I suggest, Dirzed, that one of my Assassins drives the airboat? I want you on the back seat with me, to explain the situation as we go."

Dirzed's teeth flashed white against his brown skin as he gave Verkan Vall a quick smile.

"By all means, Lord Virzal; I would much rather be distrusted than to find that my client's friends were not discreet."

There were a couple of hotel Assassins guarding Dirzed's airboat, on the landing stage. Marnik climbed in under the controls, with Olirzon beside him; Verkan Vall and Dirzed entered the rear seat. Dirzed gave Marnik the co-ordinate reference for their destination.

"Now, what sort of a place is this, where we're going?" Verkan Vall asked. "And who's there whom we may or may not trust?"

"Well, it's a dome house belonging to the family of Starpha; they own a five-mile radius around it, oak and beech forest and underbrush, stocked with deer and boar. A hunting lodge. Prince Jirzyn of Starpha, Lord Girzon of Roxor, and a few other top-level Volitionalists, know that the Lady Dallona's hiding there. They're keeping her out of sight till after the election, for propaganda purposes. We've been hiding there since immediately after the discarnation feast of the Lord Garnon of Roxor."

"What happened, after the feast?" Verkan Vall wanted to know.

"Well, you know how the Lady Dallona and Dr. Harnosh of Hosh had this telepathic-sensitive there, in a trance and drugged with a *zerfa*-derivative alkaloid the Lady Dallona had developed. I was Lord Garnon's Assassin; I discarnated him, myself. Why, I hadn't even put my pistol away before he was in control of this sensitive, in a room five stories above the banquet hall; he began communicating at once. We had visiplates to show us what was going on.

"Right away, Nirzav of Shonna, one of the Statisticalist leaders who was a personal friend of Lord Garnon's in spite of his politics, renounced Statisticalism and went over to the Volitionalists, on the strength of this communication. Prince Jirzyn, and Lord Girzon, the new family-head of Roxor, decided that there would be trouble in the next few days, so they advised the Lady Dallona to come to this hunting lodge for safety. She and I came here in her airboat, directly from the feast. A good thing we did, too; if we'd gone to her apartment, we'd have walked in before that lethal gas had time to clear.

"There are four Assassins of the family of Starpha, and six menservants, and an upper-servant named Tarnod, the gamekeeper. The Starpha Assassins and I have been keeping the rest under observation. I left one of the Starpha Assassins guarding the Lady Dallona when I came for you, under brotherly oath to protect her in my name till I returned."

The airboat was skimming rapidly above the treetops, toward the northern part of the city.

"What's known about that package bomb?" Verkan Vall asked. "Who sent it?"

Dirzed shrugged. "The Statisticalists, of course. The

wrapper was stolen from the Reincarnation Research Institute; so was the case. The Constabulary are working on it." Dirzed shrugged again.

The dome, about a hundred and fifty feet in width and some fifty in height, stood among the trees ahead. It was almost invisible from any distance; the concrete dome was of mottled green and gray concrete, trees grew so close as to brush it with their branches, and the little pavilion on the flattened top was roofed with translucent green plastic. As the airboat came in, a couple of men in Assassins' garb emerged from the pavilion to meet them.

"Marnik, stay at the controls," Verkan Vall directed. "I'll send Olirzon up for you if I want you. If there's any trouble, take off for Assassins' Hall and give the code word, then come back with twice as many men as you think you'll need."

Dirzed raised his eyebrows over this. "I hadn't known the Assassin-President had given you a code word, Lord Virzal," he commented. "That doesn't happen very often."

"The Assassin-President has honored me with his friendship," Verkan Vall replied noncommittally, as he, Dirzed and Olirzon climbed out of the airboat. Marnik was holding it an unobtrusive inch or so above the flat top of the dome, away from the edge of the pavilion roof.

The two Assassins greeted him, and a man in upper-servants' garb and wearing a hunting knife and a long hunting pistol approached.

"Lord Virzal of Verkan? Welcome to Starpha Dome. The Lady Dallona awaits you below."

Verkan Vall had never been in an Akor-Neb dwelling dome, but a description of such structures had been included in his hypno-mech indoctrination. Originally, they had been the standard structure for all purposes; about two thousand elapsed years ago, when nationalism had still existed on the Akor-Neb Sector, the cities had been almost entirely under ground, as protection from air attack. Even now, the design had been retained by those who wished to live apart from the towering city units, to preserve the natural appearance of the landscape. The Starpha hunting lodge was typical of such domes. Under it was a circular well, eighty feet in depth and fifty in width, with a fountain and a shallow circular pool at the bottom. The storerooms, kitchens and servants' quarters were at the top, the living quarters at the bottom, in segments of a wide circle around the well, back of balconies.

"Tarnod, the gamekeeper," Dirzed performed the introductions. "And Erarno and Kirzol, Assassins."

Verkan Vall hooked fingers and clapped shoulders with them. Tarnod accompanied them to the lifter tubes—two percent positive gravitation for descent and two percent negative for ascent—and they all floated down the former, like air-filled balloons, to the bottom level.

"The Lady Dallona is in the gun room," Tarnod informed Verkan Vall, making as though to guide him.

"Thanks, Tarnod; we know the way," Dirzed told him shortly, turning his back on the upper-servant and walking toward a closed door on the other side of the fountain. Verkan Vall and Olirzon followed; for a moment, Tarnod stood looking after them, then he followed the other two Assassins into the ascent tube.

"I don't relish that fellow," Dirzed explained. "The family of Starpha use him for work they couldn't hire an Assassin to do at any price. I've been here often, when I was with the Lord Garnon; I've always thought he had something on Prince Jirzyn."

He knocked sharply on the closed door with the butt of his pistol. In a moment, it slid open, and a young Assassin with a narrow mustache and a tuft of chin beard looked out.

"Ah, Dirzed." He stepped outside. "The Lady Dallona is within; I return her to your care."

Verkan Vall entered, followed by Dirzed and Olirzon.

The big room was fitted with reclining chairs and couches and low tables; its walls were hung with the heads of deer and boar and wolves, and with racks holding rifles and hunting pistols and fowling pieces. It was filled with the soft glow of indirect cold light. At the far side of the room, a young woman was seated at a desk, speaking softly into a sound transcriber. As they entered, she snapped it off and rose.

Hadron Dalla wore the same costume Verkan Vall had seen on the visiplate: he recognized her instantly. It took her a second or two to perceive Verkan Vall under the brown skin and black hair of the Lord Virzal of Verkan. Then her face lighted with a happy smile.

"Why, Va-a-a-ll!" she whooped, running across the room and tossing herself into his not particularly reluctant arms. After all, it had been twenty years—"I didn't know you, at first!"

"You mean, in these clothes?" he asked, seeing that she had forgotten, for the moment, the presence of the two Assassins. She had even called him by his First Level name, but that was unimportant—the Akor-Neb affectionate diminutive was formed by omitting the -*irz*- or -*arn*-. "Well, they're not exactly what I generally wear on the plantation." He kissed her again, then turned to his companions. "Your pardon, Gentlemen-Assassins; it's been something over a year since we've seen each other."

Olirzon was smiling at the affectionate reunion; Dirzed wore a look of amused resignation, as though he might have expected something like this to happen. Verkan Vall and Dalla sat down on a couch near the desk.

"That was really sweet of you, Vall, fighting those men for talking about me," she began. "You took an awful chance, though. But if you hadn't, I'd never have known you were in Darsh—Oh-oh! That was why you did it, wasn't it?"

"Well, I had to do something. Everybody either didn't know or weren't saying where you were. I assumed, from the circumstances, that you were hiding somewhere. Tell me, Dalla; do you really have scientific proof of reincarnation? I mean, as an established fact?"

"Oh, yes; these people on this sector have had that for over ten centuries. They have hypnotic techniques for getting back into a part of the subconscious mind that we've never been able to reach. And after I found out how they did it, I was able to adapt some of our hypno-epistemological techniques to it, and—"

"All right; that's what I wanted to know," he cut her off. "We're getting out of here, right away."

"But where?"

"Ghamma, in an airboat I have outside, and then back to the First Level. Unless there's a paratime-transposition conveyor somewhere nearer."

"But why, Vall? I'm not ready to go back; I have a lot of work to do here, yet. They're getting ready to set up a series of control-experiments at the Institute, and then, I'm in the middle of an experiment, a two-hundred-subject memory-recall experiment. See, I distributed two hundred sets of equipment for my new technique—injection-ampoules of this *zerfa*-derivative drug, and sound records of the hypnotic suggestion formula, which can be played on an ordinary reproducer. It's just a crude variant of our hypno-mech process, except that instead of implanting information in the subconscious mind, to be brought at will to the level of consciousness, it works the other way, and draws into conscious knowledge information already in the subconscious mind. The way these people have always done has been to put the subject in an hypnotic trance and then record verbal statements made in the trance state; when the subject comes out of the trance, the record is all there is, because the memories of past reincarnations have never been in the conscious mind. But with my process, the subject can consciously remember everything about his last reincarnation, and as many reincarnations before that as he wishes to. I haven't heard from any of the people who received these auto-recall kits, and I really must—"

"Dalla, I don't want to have to pull Paratime Police authority on you, but, so help me, if you don't come back voluntarily with me, I will. Security of the secret of paratime transposition."

"Oh, my eye!" Dalla exclaimed. "Don't give me that, Vall!"

"Look, Dalla. Suppose you get discarnated here," Verkan Vall said. "You say reincarnation is a scientific fact. Well, you'd reincarnate on this sector, and then you'd take a memory-recall, under hypnosis. And when you did, the paratime secret wouldn't be a secret any more."

"Oh!" Dalla's hand went to her mouth in consternation. Like every paratimer, she was conditioned to shrink with all her being from the mere thought of revealing to any out-time dweller the secret ability of her race to pass to other time-lines, or even the existence of alternate lines of probability. "And if I took one of the old-fashioned trance-recalls, I'd blat out everything; I wouldn't be able to keep a thing back. And I even know the principles of transposition!" She looked at him, aghast.

"When I get back, I'm going to put a recommendation through department channels that this whole sector be declared out of bounds for all paratime-transposition, until you people at Rhogom Foundation work out the problem of discarnate return to the First Level," he told her. "Now, have you any notes or anything you want to take back with you?"

She rose. "Yes; just what's on the desk. Find me something to put the tape spools and notebooks in, while I'm getting them in order."

He secured a large game bag from under a rack of fowling pieces, and held it while she sorted the material rapidly, stuffing spools of record tape and notebooks into it. They had barely begun when the door slid open and

Olirzon, who had gone outside, sprang into the room, his pistol drawn, swearing vilely.

"They've double-crossed us!" he cried. "The servants of Starpha have turned on us." He holstered his pistol and snatched up his submachine-gun, taking cover behind the edge of the door and letting go with a burst in the direction of the lifter tubes. "Got that one!" he grunted.

"What happened, Olirzon?" Verkan Vall asked, dropping the game bag on the table and hurrying across the room.

"I went up to see how Marnik was making out. As I came out of the lifter tube, one of the obscenities took a shot at me with a hunting pistol. He missed me; I didn't miss him. Then a couple more of them were coming up, with fowling pieces; I shot one of them before they could fire, and jumped into the descent tube and came down heels over ears. I don't know what's happened to Marnik." He fired another burst, and swore. "Missed him!"

"Assassins' Truce! Assassins' Truce!" a voice howled out of the descent tube. "Hold your fire, we want to parley."

"Who is it?" Dirzed shouted, over Olirzon's shoulder. "You, Sarnax? Come on out; we won't shoot."

The young Assassin with the mustache and chin beard emerged from the descent tube, his weapons sheathed and his clasped hands extended in front of him in a peculiarly ecclesiastical-looking manner. Dirzed and Olirzon stepped out of the gun room, followed by Verkan Vall and Hadron Dalla. Olirzon had left his submachine-gun behind. They met the other Assassin by the rim of the fountain pool.

"Lady Dallona of Hadron," the Starpha Assassin began. "I and my colleagues, in the employ of the family of Starpha, have received orders from our clients to withdraw our protection from you, and to discarnate you, and all with you who undertake to protect or support you." That much sounded like a recitation of some established formula; then his voice became more conversational. "I and my colleagues, Erarno and Kirzol and Harnif, offer our apologies for the barbarity of the servants of the family of Starpha, in attacking without declaration of cessation of friendship. Was anybody hurt or discarnated?"

"None of us," Olirzon said. "How about Marnik?"

"He was warned before hostilities were begun against him," Sarnax replied. "We will allow five minutes until—"

Olirzon, who had been looking up the well, suddenly sprang at Dalla, knocking her flat, and at the same time jerking out his pistol. Before he could raise it, a shot banged from above and he fell on his face. Dirzed, Verkan Vall, and Sarnax, all drew their pistols, but whoever had fired the shot had vanished. There was an outburst of shouting above.

"Get to cover," Sarnax told the others. "We'll let you know when we're ready to attack; we'll have to deal with whoever fired that shot, first." He looked at the dead body on the floor, exclaimed angrily, and hurried to the ascent tube, springing upward.

Verkan Vall replaced the small pistol in his shoulder holster and took Olirzon's belt, with his knife and heavier pistol.

"Well, there you see," Dirzed said, as they went back to the gun room. "So much for political expediency."

"I think I understand why your picture and the Lady Dallona's were exhibited so widely," Verkan Vall said. "Now, anybody would recognize your bodies, and blame the Statisticalists for discarnating you."

"That thought had occurred to me, Lord Virzal," Dirzed said. "I suppose our bodies will be atrociously but not unidentifiably mutilated, to further enrage the public," he added placidly. "If I get out of this carnate, I'm going to pay somebody off for it."

After a few minutes, there was more shouting of: "Assassins' Truce!" from the descent tube. The two Assassins, Erarno and Kirzol, emerged, dragging the gamekeeper, Tarnod, between them. The upper-servant's face was bloody, and his jaw seemed to be broken. Sarnax followed, carrying a long hunting pistol in his hand.

"Here he is!" he announced. "He fired during Assassins' Truce; he's subject to Assassins' Justice!"

He nodded to the others. They threw the gamekeeper forward on the floor, and Sarnax shot him through the head, then tossed the pistol down beside him. "Any more of these people who violate the decencies will be treated similarly," he promised.

"Thank you, Sarnax," Dirzed spoke up. "But we lost an Assassin: discarnating this lackey won't equalize that. We think you should retire one of your number."

"That at least, Dirzed; wait a moment."

The three Assassins conferred at some length. Then Sarnax hooked fingers and clapped shoulders with his companions.

"See you in the next reincarnation, brothers," he told them, walking toward the gun-room door, where Verkan Vall, Dalla and Dirzed stood. "I'm joining you people. You had two Assassins when the parley began, you'll have two when the shooting starts."

Verkan Vall looked at Dirzed in some surprise. Hadron Dalla's Assassin nodded.

"He's entitled to do that, Lord Virzal; the Assassins' code provides for such changes of allegiance."

"Welcome, Sarnax," Verkan Vall said, hooking fingers with him. "I hope we'll all be together when this is over."

"We will be," Sarnax assured him cheerfully. "Discarnate. We won't get out of this in the body, Lord Virzal."

A submachine-gun hammered from above, the bullets lashing the fountain pool; the water actually steamed, so great was their velocity.

"All right!" a voice called down. "Assassins' Truce is over!"

Another burst of automatic fire smashed out the

lights at the bottom of the ascent tube. Dirzed and Dalla struggled across the room, pushing a heavy steel cabinet between them; Verkan Vall, who was holding Olirzon's submachine-gun, moved aside to allow them to drop it on edge in the open doorway, then wedged the door half-shut against it. Sarnax came over, bringing rifles, hunting pistols, and ammunition.

"What's the situation, up there?" Verkan Vall asked him. "What force have they, and why did they turn against us?"

"Lord Virzal!" Dirzed objected, scandalized. "You have no right to ask Sarnax to betray confidences!"

Sarnax spat against the door. "In the face of Jirzyn of Starpha!" he said. "And in the face of his *zortan* mother, and of his father, whoever he was! Dirzed, do not talk foolishly; one does not speak of betraying betrayers." He turned to Verkan Vall. "They have three menservants of the family of Starpha; your Assassin, Olirzon, discarnated the other three. There is one of Prince Jirzyn's poor relations, named Girzad. There are three other men, Volitionalist precinct workers, who came with Girzad, and four Assassins, the three who were here, and one who came with Girzad. Eleven, against the three of us."

"The four of us, Sarnax," Dalla corrected. She had buckled on a hunting pistol, and had a light deer rifle under her arm.

Something moved at the bottom of the descent tube. Verkan Vall gave it a short burst, though it was probably only a dummy, dropped to draw fire.

"The four of us, Lady Dallona," Sarnax agreed. "As to your other Assassin, the one who stayed in the airboat, I don't know how he fared. You see, about twenty minutes ago, this Girzad arrived in an airboat, with an Assassin and these three Volitionalist workers. Erarno and I were at the top of the dome when he came in. He told us that he had orders from Prince Jirzyn to discarnate the Lady Dallona and Dirzed at once. Tarnod, the gamekeeper"—

Sarnax spat ceremoniously against the door again—"told him you were here, and that Marnik was one of your men. He was going to shoot Marnik at once, but Erarno and I and his Assassin stopped him. We warned Marnik about the change in the situation, according to the code, expecting Marnik to go down here and join you. Instead, he lifted the airboat, zoomed over Girzad's boat, and let go a rocket blast, setting Girzad's boat on fire. Well, that was a hostile act, so we all fired after him. We must have hit something, because the boat went down, trailing smoke, about ten miles away. Girzad got another airboat out of the hangar and he and his Assassin started after your man. About that time, your Assassin, Olirzon— happy reincarnation to him—came up, and the Starpha servants fired at him, and he fired back and discarnated two of them, and then jumped down the descent tube. One of the servants jumped after him; I found his body at the bottom when I came down to warn you formally. You know what happened after that."

"But why did Prince Jirzyn order our discarnation?" Dalla wanted to know. "Was it to blame the Statisticalists with it?"

Sarnax, about to answer, broke off suddenly and began firing at the opening of the ascent tube with a hunting pistol.

"I got him," he said, in a pleased tone. "That was Erarno; he was always playing tricks with the tubes, climbing down against negative gravity and up against positive gravity. His body will float up to the top—Why, Lady Dallona, that was only part of it. You didn't hear about the big scandal, on the newscast, then?"

"We didn't have it on. What scandal?"

Sarnax laughed. "Oh, the very father and family-head of all scandals! You ought to know about it, because you started it; that's why Prince Jirzyn wants you out of the body—You devised a process by which people could give themselves memory-recalls of previous reincarnations, didn't you? And distributed apparatus to do it with? And gave one set to young Tarnov, the son of Lord Tirzov of Fastor?"

Dalla nodded. Sarnax continued:

"Well, last evening, Tarnox of Fastor used his recall outfit, and what do you think? It seems that thirty years ago, in his last reincarnation, he was Jirzid of Starpha, Jirzyn's older brother. Jirzid was betrothed to the Lady Annitra of Zabna. Well, his younger brother was carrying on a clandestine affair with the Lady Annitra, and he also wanted the title of Prince and family-head of Starpha. So he bribed this fellow Tarnod, whom I had the pleasure of discarnating, and who was an underservant here at the hunting lodge. Between them, they shot Jirzid during a boar hunt. An accident, of course. So Jirzyn married the Lady Annitra, and when old Prince Jarnid, his father, discarnated a year later, he succeeded to the title. And immediately, Tarnod was made head gamekeeper here."

"What did I tell you, Lord Virzal? I knew that son of a *zortan* had something on Jirzyn of Starpha!" Dirzed exclaimed. "A nice family, this of Starpha!"

"Well, that's not the end of it," Sarnax continued. "This morning, Tarnov of Fastor, late Jirzid of Starpha, went before the High Court of Estates and entered suit to change his name to Jirzid of Starpha and laid claim to the title of Starpha family-head. The case has just been entered, so there's been no hearing, but there's the blazes of an argument among all the nobles about it—some are claiming that the individuality doesn't change from one reincarnation to the next, and others claiming that property and titles should pass along the line of physical descent, no matter what individuality has reincarnated into what body. They're the ones who want the Lady Dallona discarnated and her discoveries suppressed. And there's talk about revising the entire system of estate-ownership and estate-inheritance. Oh, it's an utter obscenity of a business!"

"This," Verkan Vall told Dalla, "is something we will not emphasize when we get home." That was as close as he dared come to it, but she caught his meaning. The working of major changes in out-time social structures was not viewed with approval by the Paratime Commission on the First Level. "*If* we get home," he added. Then an idea occurred to him.

"Dirzed, Sarnax; this place must have been used by the leaders of the Volitionalists for top-level conferences. Is there a secret passage anywhere?"

Sarnax shook his head. "Not from here. There is one, on the floor above, but they control it. And even if there were one down here, they would be guarding the outlet."

"That's what I was counting on. I'd hoped to simulate an escape that way, and then make a rush up the regular tubes." Verkan Vall shrugged. "I suppose Marnik's our only chance. I hope he got away safely."

"He was going for help? I was surprised that an Assassin would desert his client; I should have thought of that," Sarnax said. "Well, even if he got down carnate, and if Girzad didn't catch him, he'd still be afoot ten miles from the nearest city unit. That gives us a little chance—about one in a thousand."

"Is there any way they can get at us, except by those tubes?" Dalla asked.

"They could cut a hole in the floor, or burn one through," Sarnax replied. "They have plenty of thermite. They could detonate a charge of explosives over our heads, or clear out of the dome and drop one down the well. They could use lethal gas or radiodust, but their Assassins wouldn't permit such illegal methods. Or they could shoot sleep-gas down at us, and then come down and cut our throats at their leisure."

"We'll have to get out of this room, then," Verkan Vall decided. "They know we've barricaded ourselves in here; this is where they'll attack. So we'll patrol the perimeter of the well; we'll be out of danger from above if we keep close to the wall. And we'll inspect all the rooms on this floor for evidence of cutting through from above."

Sarnax nodded. "That's sense, Lord Virzal. How about the lifter tubes?"

"We'll have to barricade them. Sarnax, you and Dirzed know the layout of this place better than the Lady Dallona or I; suppose you two check the rooms, while we cover the tubes and the well," Verkan Vall directed. "Come on, now."

They pushed the door wide-open and went out past the cabinet. Hugging the wall, they began a slow circuit of the well, Verkan Vall in the lead with the submachine-gun, then Sarnax and Dirzed, the former with a heavy boar-rifle and the latter with a hunting pistol in each hand, and Hadron Dalla brought up in the rear with her rifle. It was she who noticed a movement along the rim of the balcony above and snapped a shot at it; there was a crash above, and a shower of glass and plastic and metal fragments rattled on the pavement of the court. Somebody had been trying to lower a scanner or a visiplate-pickup, or something of the sort; the exact nature of the instrument was not evident from the wreckage Dalla's bullet had made of it.

The rooms Dirzed and Sarnax entered were all quiet; nobody seemed to be attempting to cut through the ceiling, fifteen feet above. They dragged furniture from a couple of rooms, blocking the openings of the lifter tubes, and continued around the well until they had reached the gun room again.

Dirzed suggested that they move some of the weapons and ammunition stored there to Prince Jirzyn's private apartment, halfway around to the lifter tubes, so that another place of refuge would be stocked with munitions in event of their being driven from the gun room.

Leaving him on guard outside, Verkan Vall, Dalla and Sarnax entered the gun room and began gathering weapons and boxes of ammunition. Dalla finished packing her game bag with the recorded data and notes of her experiments. Verkan Vall selected four more of the heavy hunting pistols, more accurate than his shoulder-holster weapon or the dead Olirzon's belt arm, and capable of either full or semi-automatic fire. Sarnax chose a couple more boar rifles. Dalla slung her bag of recorded notes, and another bag of ammunition, and secured another deer rifle. They carried this accumulation of munitions to the private apartments of Prince Jirzyn, dumping every-thing in the middle of the drawing room, except the bag of notes, from which Dalla refused to separate herself.

"Maybe we'd better put some stuff over in one of the rooms on the other side of the well," Dirzed suggested. "They haven't really begun to come after us; when they do, we'll probably be attacked from two or three direc-tions at once."

They returned to the gun room, casting anxious glances at the edge of the balcony above and at the barri-cade they had erected across the openings to the lifter tubes. Verkan Vall was not satisfied with this last; it looked to him as though they had provided a breastwork for somebody to fire on them from, more than anything else.

He was about to step around the cabinet which par-tially blocked the gun-room door when he glanced up, and saw a six-foot circle on the ceiling turning slowly brown. There was a smell of scorched plastic. He grabbed Sarnax by the arm and pointed.

"Thermite," the Assassin whispered. "The ceiling's got six inches of spaceship-insulation between it and the floor above; it'll take them a few minutes to burn through it." He stooped and pushed on the barricade, shoving it into the room. "Keep back; they'll probably drop a gre-nade or so through, first, before they jump down. If we're quick, we can get a couple of them."

Dirzed and Sarnax crouched, one at either side of the

door, with weapons ready. Verkan Vall and Dalla had been ordered, rather peremptorily, to stay behind them; in a place of danger, an Assassin was obliged to shield his client. Verkan Vall, unable to see what was going on inside the room, kept his eyes and his gun muzzle on the barricade across the openings to the lifter tubes, the erection of which he was now regretting as a major tactical error.

Inside the gun room, there was a sudden crash, as the circle of thermite burned through and a section of ceiling dropped out and hit the floor. Instantly, Dirzed flung himself back against Verkan Vall, and there was a tremendous explosion inside, followed by another and another. A second or so passed, then Dirzed, leaning around the corner of the door, began firing rapidly into the room. From the other side of the door, Sarnax began blazing away with his rifle. Verkan Vall kept his position, covering the lifter tubes.

Suddenly, from behind the barricade, a blue-white gun flash leaped into being, and a pistol banged. He sprayed the opening between a couch and a section of bookcase from whence it had come, releasing his trigger as the gun rose with the recoil, squeezing and releasing and squeezing again. Then he jumped to his feet.

"Come on, the other place; hurry!" he ordered.

Sarnax swore in exasperation. "Help me with her, Dirzed!" he implored.

Verkan Vall turned his head, to see the two Assassins drag Dalla to her feet and hustle her away from the gun room; she was quite senseless, and they had to drag her between them. Verkan Vall gave a quick glance into the gun room; two of the Starpha servants and a man in rather flashy civil dress were lying on the floor, where they had been shot as they had jumped down from above. He saw a movement at the edge of the irregular, smoking, hole in the ceiling, and gave it a short burst, then fired another at the exit from the descent tube. Then he took to his heels and followed the Assassins and Hadron Dalla into Prince Jirzyn's apartment.

As he ran through the open door, the Assassins were letting Dalla down into a chair; they instantly threw themselves into the work of barricading the doorway so as to provide cover and at the same time allow them to fire out into the central well.

For an instant, as he bent over her, he thought Dalla had been killed, an assumption justified by his knowledge of the deadliness of Akor-Neb bullets. Then he saw her eye-lids flicker. A moment later, he had the explanation of her escape. The bullet had hit the game bag at her side; it was full of spools of metal tape, in metal cases, and notes in written form, pyrographed upon sheets of plastic ring fastened into metal binders. Because of their extreme velocity, Akor-Neb bullets were sure killers when they struck animal tissue, but for the same reason, they had very poor penetration on hard objects. The alloy-steel tape, and the steel spools and spool cases, and the note-book binders, had been enough to shatter the little bullet into splinters of magnesium-nickel alloy, and the stout leather back of the game bag had stopped all of these. But the impact, even distributed as it had been through the contents of the bag, had been enough to knock the girl unconscious.

He found a bottle of some sort of brandy and a glass on a serving table nearby and poured her a drink, holding it to her lips. She spluttered over the first mouthful, then took the glass from him and sipped the rest.

"What happened?" she asked. "I thought those bullets were sure death."

"Your notes. The bullet hit the bag. Are you all right, now?"

She finished the brandy. "I think so." She put a hand into the game bag and brought out a snarled and tangled mess of steel tape. "Oh, *blast*! That stuff was important; all the records on the preliminary auto-recall experiments." She shrugged. "Well, it wouldn't have been worth much more if I'd stopped that bullet, myself." She slipped the strap over her shoulder and started to rise.

As she did, a bedlam of firing broke out, both from the two Assassins at the door and from outside. They both hit the floor and crawled out of line of the partly-open door; Verkan Vall recovered his submachine-gun, which he had set down beside Dalla's chair. Sarnax was firing with his rifle at some target in the direction of the lifter tubes; Dirzed lay slumped over the barricade, and one glance at his crumpled figure was enough to tell Verkan Vall that he was dead.

"You fill magazines for us," he told Dalla, then crawled to Dirzed's place at the door. "What happened, Sarnax?"

"They shoved over the barricade at the lifter tubes and came out into the well. I got a couple, they got Dirzed, and now they're holed up in rooms all around the circle. They—Aah!" He fired three shots, quickly, around the edge of the door. "That stopped that." The Assassin crouched to insert a fresh magazine into his rifle.

Verkan Vall risked one eye around the corner of the doorway, and as he did, there was a red flash and a dull roar, unlike the blue flashes and sharp cracking reports of the pistols and rifles, from the doorway of the gun room. He wondered, for a split second, if it might be one of the fowling pieces he had seen there, and then something whizzed past his head and exploded with a soft *plop* behind him. Turning, he saw a pool of gray vapor beginning to spread in the middle of the room. Dalla must have got a breath of it, for she was slumped over the chair from which she had just risen.

Dropping the submachine-gun and gulping a lungful of fresh air from outside, Verkan Vall rushed to her, caught her by the heels, and dragged her into Prince Jirzyn's bedroom, beyond. Leaving her in the middle of the floor, he took another deep breath and returned to the drawing room, where Sarnax was already overcome by the sleep-gas.

He saw the serving table from which he had got the brandy, and dragged it over to the bedroom door, over-turning it and laying it across the doorway, its legs in the air. Like most Akor-Neb serving tables, it had a gravity-counteraction unit under it; he set this for double minus-gravitation and snapped it on. As it was now above the inverted table, the table did not rise, but a tendril, of sleep-gas, curling toward it, bent upward and drifted away from the doorway. Satisfied that he had made a tem-porary barrier against the sleep-gas, Verkan Vall secured Dalla's hunting pistol and spare magazines and lay down at the bedroom door.

For some time, there was silence outside. Then the besiegers evidently decided that the sleep-gas attack had been a success. An Assassin, wearing a gas mask and car-rying a submachine-gun, appeared in the doorway, and behind him came a tall man in a tan tunic, similarly masked. They stepped into the room and looked around.

Knowing that he would be shooting over a two hun-dred percent negative gravitation-field, Verkan Vall aimed for the Assassin's belt-buckle and squeezed. The bullet caught him in the throat. Evidently the bullet had not only been lifted in the negative gravitation, but lifted point-first and deflected upward. He held his front sight just above the other man's knee, and hit him in the chest.

As he fired, he saw a wisp of gas come sliding around the edge of the inverted table. There was silence outside, and for an instant, he was tempted to abandon his post and go to the bathroom, back of the bedroom, for wet towels to improvise a mask. Then, when he tried to crawl backward, he could not. There was an impression of dis-tant shouting which turned to a roaring sound in his head. He tried to lift his pistol, but it slipped from his fin-gers.

When consciousness returned, he was lying on his back, and something cold and rubbery was pressing into his face. He raised his arms to fight off whatever it was, and opened his eyes, to find that he was staring directly at the red oval and winged bullet of the Society of Assassins. A hand caught his wrist as he reached for the small pistol under his arm. The pressure on his face eased.

"It's all right, Lord Virzal," a voice came to him. "Assassins' Truce!"

He nodded stupidly and repeated the words. "Assassins' Truce; I won't shoot. What happened?"

Then he sat up and looked around. Prince Jirzyn's bedchamber was full of Assassins. Dalla, recovering from her touch of sleep-gas, was sitting groggily in a chair, while five or six of them fussed around her, getting in each others' way, handing her drinks, chaffing her wrists, holding damp cloths on her brow. That was standard procedure, when any group of males thought Dalla needed any help. Another Assassin, beside the bed, was putting away an oxygen-mask outfit, and the Assassin who had prevented Verkan Vall from drawing his pistol was his own follower, Marnik. And Klarnood, the Assassin-President, was sitting on the foot of the bed, smoking one of Prince Jirzyn's monogrammed and crested cigarettes critically.

Verkan Vall looked at Marnik, and then at Klarnood, and back to Marnik.

"You got through," he said. "Good work, Marnik; I thought they'd downed you."

"They did; I had to crash-land in the woods. I went about a mile on foot, and then I found a man and woman and two children, hiding in one of these little log rain shelters. They had an airboat, a good one. It seemed that rioting had broken out in the city unit where they lived, and they'd taken to the woods till things quieted down again. I offered them Assassins' protection if they'd take me to Assassins' Hall, and they did."

"By luck, I was in when Marnik arrived," Klarnood took over. "We brought three boatloads of men, and came here at once. Just as we got here, two boatloads of Starpha dependents arrived; they tried to give us an argument, and we discarnated the lot of them. Then we came down here, crying Assassins' Truce. One of the Starpha Assassins, Kirzol, was still carnate; he told us what had been going on." The President-General's face-became grim. "You know, I take a rather poor view of Prince Jirzyn's procedure in this matter, not to mention that of his underlings. I'll have to speak to him about this. Now, how about you and the Lady Dallona? What do you intend doing?"

"We're getting out of here," Verkan Vall said. "I'd like air transport and protection as far as Ghamma, to the establishment of the family of Zorda. Brarnend of Zorda has a private space yacht; he'll get us to Venus."

Klarnood gave a sigh of obvious relief. "I'll have you and the Lady Dallona airborne and off for Ghamma as soon as you wish," he promised. "I will, frankly, be delighted to see the last of both of you. The Lady Dallona has started a fire here at Darsh that won't burn out in a half-century, and who knows what it may consume." He was interrupted by a heaving shock that made the underground dome dwelling shake like a light airboat in turbulence. Even eighty feet under the ground, they could hear a continued crashing roar. It was an appreciable interval before the sound and the shock ceased.

For an instant, there was silence, and then an excited bedlam of shouting broke from the Assassins in the room: Klarnood's face was frozen in horror.

"That was a fission bomb!" he exclaimed. "The first one that has been exploded on this planet in hostility in a thousand years!" He turned to Verkan Vall. "If you feel well enough to walk, Lord Virzal, come with us. I must see what's happened."

They hurried from the room and went streaming up

the ascent tube to the top of the dome. About forty miles away, to the south, Verkan Vall saw the sinister thing that he had seen on so many other time-lines, in so many other paratime sectors—a great pillar of varicolored fire-shot smoke, rising to a mushroom head fifty thousand feet above.

"Well, that's it," Klarnood said sadly. "That is civil war."

"May I make a suggestion, Assassin-President?" Verkan Vall asked. "I understand that Assassins' Truce is binding even upon non-Assassins; is that correct?"

"Well, not exactly; it's generally kept by such non-Assassins as want to remain in their present reincarnations, though."

"That's what I meant. Well, suppose you declare a general, planet-wide Assassins' Truce in this political war, and make the leaders of both parties responsible for keeping it. Publish lists of the top two or three thousand Statisticalists and Volitionalists, starting with Mirzark of Bashad and Prince Jirzyn of Starpha, and inform them that they will be assassinated, in order, if the fighting doesn't cease."

"Well!" A smile grew on Klarnood's face. "Lord Virzal, my thanks; a good suggestion. I'll try it. And furthermore, I'll withdraw all Assassin protection permanently from anybody involved in political activity, and forbid any Assassin to accept any retainer connected with political factionalism. It's about time our members stopped discarnating each other in these political squabbles." He pointed to the three airboats drawn up on the top of the dome; speedy black craft, bearing the red oval and winged bullet. "Take your choice, Lord Virzal. I'll lend you a couple of my men, and you'll be in Ghamma in three hours." He hooked fingers and clapped shoulders with Verkan Vall, bent over Dalla's hand. "I still like you, Lord Virzal, and I have seldom met a more charming lady than you, Lady Dallona. But I sincerely hope I never see either of you again."

The ship for Dhergabar was driving north and west; at seventy thousand feet, it was still daylight, but the world below was wrapping itself in darkness. In the big visiscreens, which served in lieu of the windows which could never have withstood the pressure and friction heat of the ship's speed, the sun was sliding out of sight over the horizon to port. Verkan Vall and Dalla sat together, watching the blazing western sky—the sky of their own First Level time-line.

"I blame myself terribly, Vall," Dalla was saying. "And I didn't mean any of them the least harm. All I was interested in was learning the facts. I know, that sounds like 'I didn't know it was loaded,' but—"

"It sounds to me like those Fourth Level Europo-American Sector physicists who are giving themselves guilt-complexes because they designed an atomic bomb," Verkan Vall replied. "All you were interested in was learning the facts. Well, as a scientist, that's all you're supposed to be interested in. You don't have to worry about any social or political implications. People have to learn to live with newly-discovered facts; if they don't, they die of them."

"But, Vall; that sounds dreadfully irresponsible—"

"Does it? You're worrying about the results of your reincarnation memory-recall discoveries, the shootings and riotings and the bombing we saw." He touched the pommel of Olirzon's knife, which he still wore. "You're no more guilty of that than the man who forged this blade is guilty of the death of Marnark of Bashad; if he'd never lived, I'd have killed Marnark with some other knife somebody else made. And what's more, you can't know the results of your discoveries. All you can see is a thin film of events on the surface of an immediate situation, so you can't say whether the long-term results will be beneficial or calamitous.

"Take this Fourth Level Europo-American atomic bomb, for example. I choose that because we both know that sector, but I could think of a hundred other examples in other paratime areas. Those people, because of deforestation, bad agricultural methods and general mismanagement, are eroding away their arable soil at an alarming rate. At the same time, they are breeding like rabbits. In other words, each successive generation has less and less food to divide among more and more people, and, for inherited traditional and superstitious reasons, they refuse to adopt any rational program of birth-control and population-limitation.

"But, fortunately, they now have the atomic bomb, and they are developing radioactive poisons, weapons of mass-effect. And their racial, nationalistic and ideological conflicts are rapidly reaching the explosion point. A series of all-out atomic wars is just what that sector needs, to bring their population down to their world's carrying capacity; in a century or so, the inventors of the atomic bomb will be hailed as the saviors of their species."

"But how about my work on the Akor-Neb Sector?" Dalla asked. "It seems that my memory-recall technique is more explosive than any fission bomb. I've laid the train for a century-long reign of anarchy!"

"I doubt that; I think Klarnood will take hold, now that he has committed himself to it. You know, in spite of his sanguinary profession, he's the nearest thing to a real man of good will I've found on that sector. And here's something else you haven't considered. Our own First Level life expectancy is from four to five hundred years. That's the main reason why we've accomplished as much as we have. We have, individually, time to accomplish things. On the Akor-Neb Sector, a scientist or artist or scholar or statesman will grow senile and die before he's as old as either of us. But now, a young student of twenty or so can take one of your auto-recall treatments and immediately have available all the knowledge and experience gained in four or five previous lives. He can start where he left off in his last reincarnation. In other words, you've made those people time-binders, individually as well as racially. Isn't that worth the temporary discarnation of a lot of ward-heelers and plug-uglies, or even a few decent types like Dirzed and Olirzon? If it isn't, I don't know what scales of values you're using."

"Vall!" Dalla's eyes glowed with enthusiasm. "I never thought of that! And you said, 'temporary discarnation.' That's just what it is. Dirzed and Olirzon and the others aren't dead; they're just waiting, discarnate, between physical lives. You know, in the sacred writings of one of the Fourth Level peoples it is stated: 'Death is the last enemy.' By proving that death is just a cyclic condition of continued individual existence, these people have conquered their last enemy."

"Last enemy but one," Verkan Vall corrected. "They still have one enemy to go, an enemy within themselves. Call it semantic confusion, or illogic, or incomprehension, or just plain stupidity. Like Klarnood, stymied by verbal objections to something labeled 'political intervention.' He'd never have consented to use the power of his Society if he hadn't been shocked out of his inhibitions by that nuclear bomb. Or the Statisticalists, trying to create a classless order of society through a political program which would only result in universal servitude to an omnipotent government. Or the Volitionalist nobles, trying to preserve their hereditary feudal privileges, and now they can't even agree on a definition of the term 'hereditary.' Might they not recover all the silly prejudices of their past lives, along with the knowledge and wisdom?"

"But ... I thought you said—" Dalla was puzzled, a little hurt.

Verkan Vall's arm squeezed around her waist, and he laughed comfortingly.

"You see? Any sort of result is possible, good or bad. So don't blame yourself in advance for something you can't possibly estimate." An idea occurred to him, and he straightened in the seat. "Tell you what; if you people at Rhogom Foundation get the problem of discarnate para-time transposition licked by then, let's you and I go back to the Akor-Neb Sector in about a hundred years and see what sort of a mess those people have made of things."

"A hundred years: that would be Year Twenty-Two of the next millennium. It's a date, Vall; we'll do it."

They bent to light their cigarettes together at his lighter. When they raised their heads again and got the flame glare out of their eyes, the sky was purple-black, dusted with stars, and dead ahead, spilling up over the horizon, was a golden glow—the lights of Dhergabar and home.

www.ingramcontent.com/pod-product-compliance
Lightning Source LLC
Chambersburg PA
CBHW052141170626
46812CB00004B/1536